Praise for

CHURCHILL'S CAT: A FELINE REMEMBRANCE

"Churchill's Cat is an enchanting and charming book. All cat lovers and fans of Winston Churchill will love it – and understand it. I loved it."
Cita Stelzer
Author of *Dinner with Churchill:
Policy Making at the Dinner Table*

"Churchill's Cat certainly gives readers a unique angle, and I was surprised at how quickly and thoroughly it drew me into Churchill's world."
Dr. Allen Packwood
Author of *How Churchill Waged War*
Director, Churchill Archives Centre, Cambridge

"Churchill's Cat is an incredible exercise in both empathy and understanding which will fascinate cat lovers and Churchill admirers alike."
Dr. Piers Brendon
Author of *Churchill's Bestiary: His Life Thru Animals*
Former Director, Churchill Archives Centre, Cambridge

"A most enjoyable book that gives an intriguing look at life at Churchill's Chartwell."
David Riddle
Former National Trust Volunteer at Chartwell

"What a loving portrayal of both the man and his cat! The emotional bonds in this book grow, not only between Winston and his cat, but also between the reader and the two main characters."

Cheryl Servais
Cat lover and world traveler

"The cat's point of view shows us a side of Churchill not often seen. A delightful and moving work of historical fiction."

Heather Gregory
Detective Inspector (Ret.)
London Metropolitan Police Service

"Your book is a delight and wonderful read. You captured the essence of both Sir Winston and his devoted cat, a skillful accomplishment."

Thomas F. Gede
Attorney at Law, San Francisco, California

"*Churchill's Cat* reveals new insights about Winston Churchill's final years. A perfect blend of history and storytelling."

G. Dulany Howland
Wealth Manager and
Director Emeritus, Harvard Club of Dallas

Praise for

CHURCHILL Without Blood, Sweat, or Tears: Applying His Methods for Today's Leaders

"A great, little Churchill book! The book is beautifully done."
Randolph Spencer Churchill
Great grandson of Sir Winston Churchill
President, International Churchill Society

"Both Lincoln and Churchill had their leadership forged in crisis. Larry Kryske's unique leadership perspective reveals Churchill's approach for a new generation of leaders."
Donald T. Phillips
Author of *Lincoln on Leadership for Today*

"No one is better qualified to write on this subject…This brief, brisk, and powerful handbook is informed by a lifetime of study and experience and is highly recommended…"
Dr. David Freeman
Director of Publications, Intl Churchill Society

"Kryske has written a tour de force on Churchill's leadership techniques, explored inside and out, and made them accessible for ready application."
William John Shepherd
Review in *The Churchill Project*, Hillsdale College

"This book is an excellent guide to using the accomplishment of Churchill's life and applying his leadership success techniques to your own."
Jonathan Thomas
Review in *Anglotopia: Magazine for Anglophiles*

"Commander Kryske is the right person to share the leadership of Winston Churchill. He demonstrated great leadership, professionalism, and dedication throughout his naval career."
Gene Taylor, Congressman,
U.S. House of Representatives (1989-2011)

"Once again Larry Kryske is back to uncover more about Winston Churchill, one of the most effective and inspirational leaders of all time. Larry's knowledge and experience as a leader make him unusually qualified to relate Churchill's wisdom to 21st century leaders."
Dr. James E. Auer
Director, Auer U.S. – Japan Center,
Professor Emeritus, Vanderbilt University

"A quick read! The leadership concepts are understandable and readily applicable. This book delivers more than it promises!"
John Henry King
Economic Development Director
City of Bowie, Maryland

CHURCHILL'S CAT
A Feline Remembrance

BOOKS BY LARRY KRYSKE

Nonfiction:

CHURCHILL Without Blood, Sweat, or Tears:
Applying His Methods for Today's Leaders
(2018)

Ready, BEGIN! Practical Strategies for
Cultivating Courage (2008)

The Greatest Board in the World: How an
Association's Board Became an Extraordinary
Team and Created a Winning Association
(2004)

The Churchill Factors: Creating Your Finest
Hour (2000)

CHURCHILL'S CAT

CAT
A Feline Remembrance

Larry Kryske

HOMEPORT PUBLISHING

**HOMEPORT
PUBLISHING**

YourFinestHour.com

Dedicated to:

**Kyle, Jeff, Paul K,
Julie, and Paul G**

**Of whom I am
so incredibly proud!**

Contents

Introduction

THE sixteenth-century French philosopher Michel de Montaigne presented a paradox that confronts anyone dealing with cats. He said, "When I play with my cat, how do I know that she is not playing with me rather than I with her?" In other words, truly getting into a cat's mind is impossible, and when you do attempt it, you face the dilemma that you are compelled to characterize it in human terms.

In this book the cat protagonist thinks human thoughts as well as feline ones. This anthropomorphic attribute gives *Churchill's Cat* its uniqueness. Borrowing from Churchill's quotation concerning Russia, one might say a cat is "a riddle, wrapped in a mystery, inside an enigma."

As in any work of fiction, the reader will have to indulge in what the nineteenth-century English poet Samuel Taylor Coleridge called the "willing suspension of disbelief," in effect, a leap of literary faith. This incredulity represents the small price that readers are required to pay for the sake of enjoyment.

The purpose of *Churchill's Cat: A Feline Remembrance* is threefold. First, it illuminates the true story of Winston Churchill's last years. This period is less well known, and rightfully so, considering his involvement in Victorian wars, the First World War, his wilderness years, the Second World War, and the Cold War. Second, it reveals the origin of the charming Chartwell tradition of always having a marmalade cat with white bib and socks. Finally, it reminds people of Churchill's legacy as one of the greatest leaders and statesmen of the twentieth century.

Prologue

I was Winston Churchill's last pet. He loved animals of all kinds, from black swans to his golden orfe. He had an especially close relationship with his beloved poodles Rufus and Rufus II, Toby his budgie, and his cats Mickey, Tango, Nelson, Smoky, Whiskey, Gabriel, and Ginger. None of them, however, shared their memories of him.

This weighty duty has been left for me, and being a stand-up creature, I readily accept the responsibility. A vast menagerie of animals encircling my human have had the lion's heart. It has fallen to me to express the roar.

Chapter 1

The Grand Alliance

"WE'RE now approaching Hyde Park Gate," my rescuer said.

I couldn't see it since I was in a box on the seat next to him, but I could tell that we were moving. I waited for him to describe our destination.

"It's Sir Winston Churchill's London home," he continued. "It's actually two adjoining brick-fronted townhouses in an elegant section of town.

"We're here because it's almost winter. He goes to Chartwell, his country home and favorite residence, for the summer and a couple of months on either side. That's a much larger house and sits in an extensive wooded area with gardens and lakes.

"I know you won't understand what I'm saying, but I want to tell you something about your new owner. He was the savior of our nation during its darkest hour."

I listened to his words. He didn't sound like the humans in the garden where I grew up. He had an educated voice, refined and clipped in speech, deep with a hesitant manner of talking. But his tone was soft and calming, just what I needed to hear.

"I worked for him during two premierships, and I continue to see him as a friend. He's getting on in years and no longer has the strength or energy to do as much as he used to do," my rescuer informed.

I waited as he collected his thoughts.

"He was once a thrilling speaker, but he's now reduced to short phrases. He was also the master of the written word. Still, you'll be a fly on the wall with the greatest living Englishman."

He must mean that I'll have the cat-on-the-carpet view.

"My friend truly loves animals. He recently lost his pet bird, Toby, who flew out an open window and never returned."

Too bad, I thought. He was probably tasty.

He paused. "Nothing could console him, and I could tell he missed his pet. Humans get terribly attached to their pets. It's a bond unlike any other.

"Winston's not as talkative as I am, but he'll be the one to give you your name. I must confess I'm curious what it will be."

Finally we came to a stop.

"We're here," he said. "By the way, your life is going to be much better now that I've freed you from the shelter, and so is his. Be at your best, Mr. Cat; prove to me that you are worthy of this deliverance."

With that guidance, I felt my box being lifted up. I was jostled around as the box was carried forward.

The man rang a doorbell. Someone answered and said, "Good afternoon, sir. He's expecting you in the drawing room."

The box moved again and then was set on what I'd later recognize as a table. I could smell smoke permeating the air in the room. It was more aromatic than the burning leaves in the large garden where I grew up. It wasn't an unpleasant smell, but it caused me to sneeze.

My rescuer spoke. "Winston, Clementine, good afternoon. And Mary, what a pleasant surprise! Nice to see you again."

"Jock Colville, I'm delighted to see you, too," Mary replied. "What do you have in the box?"

"Winston, remember the other evening when we were having dinner? Over soup I mentioned that you were without a pet."

I heard a short grunt of approval.

"And I suggested you get another," he continued. "Then I asked if you'd accept a kitten."

Winston spoke. "Indeed, I would, I said." His voice was strong and resonant.

"Happy birthday, Winston!" Colville exclaimed.

The next thing I knew, the top of the box was opened, and two delicate hands with long, thin fingers reached in and extracted me. I was staring into the pink, cherubic face of a human wearing a tired but excited expression. He held a short, squat twig between his full lips, and smoke slowly wafted upward from it. So this was Winston.

He held me firmly if not a little too tightly. My claws sprang out instinctively. I scratched his hands and arms in self-protection for the rough handling I was receiving. He didn't seem to mind.

"Oh, he's such an energetic little cat, isn't he?" said Mary, Winston's daughter.

And then I suddenly stopped. His hands smelled like the blissfully scented lavender bush I adored so much from the garden where I grew up.

I relaxed, submitting to that calming scent, and went limp in his hands. He sensed the change, too. I was no longer resisting, and his hands loosened around me.

"Papa, what a charming marmie!" Mary proclaimed. "Just look at him! His ears look too big for him, but it's because he's only just a kitten."

Winston beamed as he held me, as if admiring a new toy.

Mary continued. "His eyes are yellow with a touch of green in them. What a pretty face—it looks like milk splashed on his cheek. And he's smiling, too."

I wasn't, but if they thought so, things might go better for me.

"I see a white V-for-victory bib on his chest as well as four white socks on his paws," Clementine, Winston's wife, joined in.

A big grin filled Winston's face. His blue eyes twinkled with delight.

"Jock, he's perfect," he replied, turning to Colville. "In fact, I will call him, 'Jock,' after you and your thoughtfulness."

Colville revealed, "He's a most lucky cat. I arrived at the shelter in the nick of time, saving him literally from the jaws of death."

Once again my rescuer hesitated then continued his story. "I don't know how he could stand all the barking I heard."

He got that right. It went on without stopping all day and night. No peace was imaginable. The best I could manage were short catnaps, each occasion being jolted awake by a dog's snarling or piercing yelp.

"The RSPCA was just minutes away from putting him down when I first saw him."

I heard Clementine say softly to herself, "The Royal Society for the Prevention of Cruelty to Animals. Indeed!"

I was surprised to hear her bitterness.

"Poor thing," Mary interjected.

"But he still has another eight lives to live out," Mr. Jock concluded.

Winston looked at me and said, "You are a beautiful pussy cat. You really are."

I squirmed a bit, wanting to be set on the table, or even better, on the ground where I could make a graceful exit.

He grabbed me a little tighter saying, "No, don't go now."

Clementine had been quietly sitting and watching as the drama unfolded. Now she stood up, reached over, squeezed her husband's arm, and said with her voice rising with enthusiasm, "Oh, Winston. He's the best birthday present. And he likes you, too."

"You're right, Kat," he admitted.

My ears perked up. Why did he call her that? Was she the top cat here?

After an instant, she turned to my rescuer and said, "Jock, thank you for bringing this joy into Winston's life."

Meanwhile, I struggled to be released, and he finally placed me on the table. He studied my gaunt, bedraggled look and asked, "Are you hungry?"

Without waiting for an answer, he told one of the housemaids who attended him, "He looks starved. Open a tin of sardines and put it in a bowl. Quick, now."

My meal arrived, and he pushed the bowl in front of me. The fish smelled wonderful, and after checking to make sure it was safe, I commenced eating nice chunks of oily meat, my tail standing tall. I forgot about Winston, Clementine, Mary, and Mr. Jock, because I was completely focused on filling my tummy with this satisfying feast.

When the bowl was empty, my pink tongue swept around cleaning drops of oil off my whiskers. Then I took a moment to study my surroundings.

Winston sat in an armchair with faded pink covers. To his left several logs blazed in a fireplace. Every now and then the fire crackled or sputtered as sap ignited. I stood on the oval table at his right hand. Clementine sat on the other side of the fireplace in an armchair with a high straight back and side wings. Mr. Jock and Mary sat next to each other, their smaller chairs facing the hearth.

Two large bookcases, replete with what I learned were leather-bound books, many written by Winston, stood on either side of a large window that fronted the garden. Radiators under the window combined with the heat from the burning logs to produce a warm atmosphere that was very pleasing to me. I prefer to be warm rather than cool or even cold. I'm sure I'll sleep better here than outside in the garden where my life began.

Afterward, I considered what I had seen, heard, and tasted. I have a name, Jock, with a ring of nobility to it. I have new friends, and I have a full stomach.

Thankfully, I was named after a favorite human instead of tritely being christened "Marmalade" or "Fluffy." I simply cannot be called something a human consumes. To be named for a person whom my human values is much better.

I also know that Winston is respected, loved, and caring. If he learns to handle me more gently, perhaps we'll get along.

Chapter 2

My Early Life

ONCE again, I'm forced to adapt to a new situation. Fortunately, cats are agile creatures who can dance with changing circumstances, and I'm no exception. I also value my independence more than anything else. I want to do what I want, when I want.

At this point in our affiliation, Winston knows virtually nothing about me, and I certainly know even less about him. Has he ever had a cat before? We're unique animals, and my early life no doubt molded me into the cat I am today.

The past, however, is a quandary for cats. We live in the now, not in the future and certainly not in the past. We're totally spontaneous. When our tummies growl, we look for food. When our bodies feel tired, we want to curl up and nap. When we feel curious, we explore.

Humans, on the other hand, live mostly in the past—past glories, past dreams, past regrets. Some live in the future, and only a few live in the present. Thus, cats and humans react differently when it comes to living their lives. I, of course, think cats are the saner of the two.

Humans cannot undo the past but still seem to spend an inordinate amount of time trying to fix what didn't work out right in their lives. Cats, on the other hand, simply live their lives adjusting as best they can to the challenges that present themselves. We adapt to varying situations, and that makes for an interesting, adventurous, and fulfilling existence.

Although cats live in the present, we do remember significant events that occurred in the past and people who were good or bad to us.

Like human children, we can't read or write. We have to memorize things we hear that are important to us. That's part of our survival. We live in a binary world of predators and prey. If we don't excel in this arena, we'll fall victim to some dog, hawk, or car.

Typically, we remember instances when we experienced extreme emotions, such as fear, love, anger, or pleasure. Getting chased by an irrational mongrel, kicked by an irate human, or honored by an especially tasty morsel of food are all occasions for remembrance.

Being in Winston's house was stressful, full of new sounds, smells, and humans. I'm not skittish, but I'm not outgoing either. I'll need to become accustomed to this different environment and see if I can trust Winston and the other humans here.

I do miss the large, secluded garden with my mother, two siblings, and the kindly woman who gave us food.

We occupied an abandoned shed in a grassy area behind a modest house. At first, the humans rarely ventured near us. Nor did any dogs come exploring, although we sometimes heard barking in the distance at night.

A high stone wall surrounded the property. A small opening in the deteriorated barrier allowed us egress to our humble abode. Our shelter kept us dry and safe. When the days and nights, however, got progressively cooler, the sun seemed to sink below the horizon earlier in the afternoon.

The woman who lived at the other end of our large garden arrived one afternoon. She was the first human I had met. She spoke gently and moved slowly so as to not frighten us. Mother, who must have had prior associations with humans, walked over to her and rubbed against her legs. The woman reached down and stroked her behind her ears. We could hear Mother's deep purring.

The human then came over to where we three kittens sat. She gently touched each of us. Then the human said, "I bet you're hungry. I'll be right back."

She returned shortly with a bowl containing scraps of fish. We all tucked in and devoured this incredible meal. It was much better than a small bird or vole.

The human returned each day bringing us something to eat. We felt comfortable enough with her that we would crawl all over her when she sat down on the grass. While we enjoyed the food treats, we didn't feel compelled to follow her to her house. We simply maintained a peaceful coexistence with her.

I soon discovered that not all humans were friendly. This human's male companion apparently did not like us intruding in his plot. He was loud and menacing. He shouted at the other human, "I think we should put them all in a sack and give them a swimming lesson in a nearby pond!" When I heard the antagonistic tone, I cowered behind Mother with my ears flattened over my head and my tail tucked beneath me.

The woman replied, "Don't you dare, or else!" This was sufficient to keep the man away. He stomped off in anger, and the woman continued to feed us every day.

One afternoon as I was exploring the other end of the lawn, I found a hedge of the most wonderful smelling plants. Shoots of small purple flowers branched out from delicate gray-green leaves. A soothing scent emanated from the flowers. Subsequently I would learn that they were called lavender. I simply could not imagine a better smell except that of Mother when she used to feed us.

The bushes were close to the human's house. Every day I returned to that scented shrub. I often dreamed about frolicking with my two siblings on a warm, sunny day with cottony white clouds dancing across a deep blue sky. I was sound asleep when the net encircled my body.

I instantly came awake! All four of my legs were in motion but to no avail. The net was connected to a long pole, and a human lifted me high into the air. Despite my best efforts, I could not escape.

There, next to my captor, was the woman's man. A look of satisfaction was spread across his cruel face. The net man quickly retrieved the pole, grabbed my squirming form by the scruff as I tried to claw his gloved hand, and thrust me roughly into a portable cage. I hissed and whined, but I was trapped.

I shook with fear as the man lifted the cage and carried me to a strange box-like creature atop wheels. I shuddered when the cage landed deafeningly on the floor inside and jumped when the door was slammed shut.

I meowed for Mother and my siblings as we drove away, but I never saw them again.

Chapter 3

The World Crisis

LATER that day, I found myself in a long, faintly-lit room with many cages. Other cats meowed and rustled around. From a nearby room, I heard a cacophony of agitated and scared dogs. My heart beat rapidly. It's impossible to experience harmony when you are so frightened and difficult to snooze with so much noise.

My cage was hard and uncomfortable. It was small, making it difficult for me to stretch. I had a bowl with water and another one with dreadfully tasting dried food. A box filled with sand sat against the side wall.

No grass, no open skies, no fragrant bushes, no brother and sister, and no Mother. I was alone. I didn't feel like eating, but eventually my growling tummy decided to submit to what was offered.

I overheard the humans who fed me talking about how vicious I was. According to the human who called the shelter and reported me, I was a feral cat who had been terrorizing him and his wife by biting and scratching them and tearing up their bushes. Therefore, despite my being a juvenile, I was not a candidate for rehoming.

I was completely unable to mark the passage of time. The dim lights always remained on. I could not see or feel the sun or observe the trees swaying in the wind. I was homesick and scared. As hard as I tried, I could not fall into a deep enough sleep to get away from my predicament.

My life had been reduced to a small cage surrounded by other cats in the same situation. Occasionally humans removed them from their cages with a noose and took them away. These cats never returned.

Once the same two humans who fed me paused near my cage. The taller, older one was explaining to the younger one about taking me to something called the "lethal chamber."

"He's been here ten days, and since he's so wild, we'll have to put him down. No one would want him as a pet."

"What exactly do we do?" asked the younger human.

"We have a small zinc-coated steel chamber with a viewing port on the front. We'll noose the cat and place him inside the chamber. Then we'll introduce about a teaspoon of chloroform onto the cotton wool pad. The open vent will let the chloroform waft into the chamber making the cat drift off to sleep."

"Is that enough chloroform to cause death?"

"No, the cat only falls asleep. After a few minutes, we'll place a lethal dose of chloroform on the pad and close all the vents. Finally, after we verify signs of death, we'll dispose of it. Simple and painless."

As I listened to them, I didn't like the sound of those words! They scared me.

Later the two humans stopped again in front of my cage.

"He doesn't look feral, does he?"

"You'd be surprised. One minute they're quiet and peaceful and the next their claws emerge and carve you up."

"Tomorrow's the day, right? Should we give him some extra food tonight, you know, a last supper?"

"No, we can't really afford to do that for any of our animals. You can watch the procedure tomorrow, and then you'll be on your own next time."

The younger one stood a while longer as the taller one walked off. He looked at me sadly.

"I wish I could let you go," he confessed. "You simply don't look like a mean cat. I'm sure someone could make a good pet out of you."

Then he shrugged his shoulders and walked off. I licked my left paw and groomed my face. I felt so dirty in this cage. No amount of grooming, however, made me feel better.

In the morning I was given a smaller amount of food than usual. I picked at it, stretched, and lay down. The humans walked over with a smaller cage and set it down beside my humble abode. The younger one carried a short pole with a leather noose on the end of it.

The older human said, "You hook him when I crack open his cage door a bit. Watch out! He's fast, and we don't want him to get away."

I saw the pole coming through the cage door and reached with my right paw to swat it away. I hissed, and my claws were at the ready. Unfortunately, the human was faster than I was and secured the noose around my neck.

As they extracted me from the cage, I tried to claw them with all my strength. I hissed and spat. A cat will fight for his life with unbelievable power, courage, and resolve.

My heart was racing, and the snare was choking me. The younger human put me into the smaller carrying cage, released the noose, and extracted the pole as the older one slammed the cage door shut. I charged and hit the cage door solidly with my body, but it didn't budge.

The younger human carried my cage as we exited the cattery. The dogs beyond seemed especially noisy and excited. Out in the hall a man was in a heated discussion with a woman with a shrill voice.

"I'd like to adopt a kitten for a friend; I hope one who'd otherwise be destroyed. Hello! Who's this?" the man inquired, pointing at my cage. He looked inside and studied me. "He'll do handsomely. I'll take this ginger fellow."

"You don't want him, sir. He's a feral cat with a nasty reputation. As we speak, he's headed for euthanizing. There are so many other well deserving cats you can choose for your friend."

"He looks perfectly fine to me." He stuck his fingers though the cage grating, but I didn't react. The human's voice wasn't aggressive.

"Sir, you shouldn't do that!" the woman insisted.

I was curious, so I sat still and looked attentive, my ears upright.

"Can't you see that he's fine? Probably just frightened. I'll take him."

Reluctantly, the humans transferred me to a small cardboard box after the man signed some papers and paid for me. It was dark inside the box, but surprisingly I wasn't scared. Happily, my rescuer had better plans for me—a new human and a new home.

Winston's London house is like being in a true shelter. There are no yelping dogs or yowling cats here and no sinister whispers from the humans. And there are no tiny cages! Only this round, pink man has handled me.

There are many new and unusual sounds—different voices, humans wheezing or coughing, people coming and going, doors opening and closing, footsteps approaching and retreating, as well as hissing logs. The wind and rain striking against the windows cause me to wince until I recognize them. My body is demanding slumber, but I dare not relax entirely until I know I'm safe.

Chapter 4

The Age of Revolution

WINSTON finally drifted off to sleep, leaving me free to roam and investigate my new surroundings. I padded around slowly, my curiosity being tempered by caution. As a result of my recent experiences, I'm wary.

I've never been in a house before. There are no trees, bushes, grass, or stone walls inside. Instead there are couches, chairs, and tables. Useless pieces of furniture hang on the walls, giving the illusion of trees, fields, and other humans. Carpet and hardwood flooring cover the ground. Peculiar sapling-like structures with narrow single trunks have a glowing brilliance at the top like the sun. Flowers sprout from unusual, clear, water- filled rocks.

Alien smells make me wrinkle my nose. They range from the smoke-like aroma that dominates the rooms that Winston occupies to the burning logs in the fireplace to a musty dryness of couches and carpets. The air is warmer than the cool freshness of an early morning outdoors.

There's a long narrow entrance hall just beyond the drawing room which opens into a study consisting of a long couch, a couple of padded chairs, some shelves with a lamp, and more framed objects on the walls. No noteworthy scents catch my attention.

I discover a connecting hall that changes direction in several places, and I guardedly follow it. It brings me to what must be Winston's bedroom. His smell lingers strongly in here, as does the odor of stale smoke. I jump up on a bed. It's soft and comfortable. Since it's perched above the floor, it could be a safe place to take a nap. None of the rooms I've visited, however, are as warm as the one where he has fallen asleep.

I return to the connecting hall when my nose detects an aroma of food. My stomach growls because I am still hungry. Following the scent leads me downstairs via a gracefully curved staircase into the basement, where the kitchen is located.

Since the humans there seem unconcerned by my sudden appearance, I approach. One of the younger ones sees me, places something on a small plate, and puts it on the floor near me. I sniff it, and then my tongue darts out to give it a taste. Its flavor resembles a bird I have caught but with a less wild tang. I devour it ravenously.

A short distance away a glazed sliding door opens to a pantry. It's warm, private, and ostensibly safe in there, a perfect place to take a snooze. I walk in, lie down, curl up my body, and fall asleep.

Evidently Winston wants me to be with him. On each occasion when I try to find a nice place to get away from his watchful eye and the smoke of his cigar, he sends his minions on a search-and-retrieve mission to bring me back. He says, "Where's the ginger?"

Then one of the young housemaids locates and returns me to him in the drawing room, where he parks himself.

"He's the master," she explains. "And he wants to hold you."

An older and wiser woman who was visiting made an aside to me. "The first time you meet Winston," she said, "you see all his faults, and the rest of your life you spend in discovering his virtues."

However, I'm still suspicious. I have claws, but I've decided not to use them because when I stay still, he rubs me gently and speaks softly to me. He has even begun calling me "Darling," elevating me above my given name. Perhaps I should appreciate him and his gestures more. He seems sincere.

His hands, perfumed with that delightful scent, nonetheless continue to squeeze me, and I wriggle to be set free. He's eager to lavish affection on me, but I'm not keen to receive it or reciprocate.

As soon as he falls asleep, I jump off his lap and slink away to the safety of my hiding place in the kitchen. There I'll catnap undisturbed until someone finds me again.

It seems like I haven't been sleeping very long when I'm recaptured and brought to the back door and deposited in the garden. Outdoors the air is refreshingly cooler and the daylight not as bright.

I don't get a chance to explore all the smells. They expect me to do my business on command so I can be returned to Winston. They are lucky I have no desire to bolt. It would have been easy to get over the fence that surrounds the garden and be gone. Nobody would be able to stop me!

But I don't know what's on the other side of the fence, so I'll stay put for now. There is food here, and nothing is more important than that. The humans seem welcoming, and Winston's lap is comfortable when his hands are preoccupied with gesturing, drinking, and smoking.

I may be a captive, but I seem to be under the influence of a benevolent dictator. I no longer seek to revolt against his actions but rather to get him to moderate them. Some might think we'll both have to reach some middle ground, but cats are not compromisers. I'll have to train this human.

Chapter 5

Step by Step

MY life has assumed a predictable set of activities—walking, standing, sitting, lying down, running, jumping, eating, and sleeping. Eating is my favorite. A person who feeds a cat is most beloved.

The biggest portion of my life is spent asleep. This enables me to recharge my strength to be in top hunting condition. However, since the human provides food, I can redirect more of my energies to exploring the extent of my new realm.

I also spend many of my waking hours observing my human, looking for my next meal, and waiting for an opportunity to go outside. A cat is always watching! Only Winston's bodyguard, Sergeant Edmund Murray of New Scotland Yard, known as the "Sergeant," is as watchful as I am.

An attentive cat is also judging time. A cat lives the Greek concept of *kairos*—propitious or opportune time—for example, when to eat, when to play, when to catnap—instead of *chronos*—

elapsed time. Clocks and calendars mean nothing to me.

Winston insists that I be at his beck and call like everyone else in the household. I typically don't come when he, or anyone else for that matter, calls me. That's not a cat's way.

And just as he refers to his secretaries by descriptions rather than by name, such as the "young woman," "redhead" or "tall Miss with hazel eyes," he initially called me "Ginger," "Pussycat," "Mr. Cat," and "Yellow Cat," but rarely, "Jock."

Accordingly, I, too, have several names for him including, "Winston," "my human," and the "big man."

I'm feeling more comfortable in his home. There are many tall perches where I can jump off the floor and then recline with my back legs outstretched, my tail still, and my front paws tucked in beneath me.

Meals have become special moments. Initially, I was a bit standoffish and avoided the big man. I hid from him as often as I could. Housemaids fed me canned cat food that smelled good but was tasteless. I gobbled it up only because I had to replace the weight I lost during captivity at the shelter.

As I became more relaxed around my human, I was invited to eat with him. Winston would allow me to jump up on his bed and share what he was eating. Naturally I was curious and would touch, sniff, and taste the unusual new offerings. I was more attracted by the food than the man, but he soon cast his spell on me.

"Good morning, Mr. Cat," he'd say cheerfully. His gold-rimmed reading glasses were perched on the end of his nose. Tilting his head downward, he looked at me over the smudged round lenses.

I reciprocated by nudging his hand and turning on my motor. A purring cat usually makes humans happy, but he could often be melancholy, brooding, or gloomy.

He then confided in me, saying in a quiet but exasperated voice, "I have achieved a great deal in my life only to have achieved nothing in the end."

I studied his pink face and noticed lines of regret around his eyes.

I learned to enjoy breakfast with Winston. He ate well. He might have a piece of steak, lamb cutlet, fried chicken leg, or scrambled eggs. On other occasions he would dab his finger in black cherry jam and hold it in front of me. I smelled the exotic scent then stuck out my tongue and licked it off his finger. I don't have a sweet tooth, but I came to enjoy this offered treat.

I liked spending the morning in bed with him. He read several newspapers. When I thought he was paying too much attention to them, I'd swat the lower edge of the paper with my paw. It became a game. He would try to lift the lower edge away from me, and I'd reach up higher to catch it. He'd chuckle and say, "Nice try, Yellow Cat. Got you that time."

After Winston has completed his reading, countless sheets of newspapers, some smudged with jam, littered the floor and needed to be cleaned up.

Then, speaking to no one in particular, Winston recited some stanzas by one of his favorite poets, Rudyard Kipling.

> "Then it's Tommy this, an' Tommy that,
> an' "Tommy, 'ow's yer soul?"
> But it's "Thin red line of 'eroes" when the
> drums begin to roll,
> The drums begin to roll, my boys, the
> drums begin to roll,
> O it's "Thin red line of 'eroes" when the
> drums begin to roll.

"For it's Tommy this, an' Tommy that,
an' Chuck him out, the brute!"
But it's Saviour of 'is country when
the guns begin to shoot;
An' it's Tommy this, an' Tommy that, an'
anything you please;
An 'Tommy ain't a bloomin' fool - you
bet that Tommy sees!"

A buoyant look filled Winston's face.

His male nurse Roy Howells also served as what Winston called "his man," a personal attendant or manservant who dressed him, monitored his health, and did any number of routine tasks for him. The big man worked him long hours. Winston was always demanding, except of me and his wife. I'm not sure where Roy found the fortitude and patience, but he was thoroughly devoted to Winston, although not overly friendly to me.

I am fascinated by Winston's different furs. Some are plusher and have different colors. I particularly like his green velvet siren suit because it is so fur-like. He likes it, too, and once shouted, "Get me my siren suit, Howes!"

Shaking his head, Roy muttered in a low voice, "I've worked for this man over four years, and he still can't get my name right. I'm Howells, not Howes!"

Mornings started on Winston's bed, but after breakfast and newspapers, I could expect a housemaid to pick me up and carry me to the garden-side door. I enjoyed these breaks that coincided with Roy's arrival to get Winston dressed.

Afterward, I sit outside Winston's door until the clock chimes at least twelve times. I know he will eventually appear and move slowly toward the drawing room for a libation prior to his midday meal. I liked to lead the parade, walking a couple paces ahead of him with my tail confidently held high.

He would sit in his chair and enjoy his drink. I lay on the carpet at his feet. When his drink was finished, he'd walk to the lift and sit in the enclosed chair.

The first time this happened, he patted his lap and said, "Mr. Cat, ready to ride downstairs?"

I refused to move. Then one of the attendants scooped me up and set me on him. I didn't like being confined in a small place. The elevator barely contained his chair! My claws came out, and I sprang for the opening.

I heard Winston say something like, "It's okay, let him go," which they did.

Once I'd heard the elevator grind and watched him disappear, I headed down the stairs and met him as he emerged on the basement level near the dining room. I liked this room not only for the food but because it opened onto the garden. I sat on one of the lower steps until all the humans were seated at the table. Then I made my presence known with a little meow.

A housemaid would bring my food bowl—the one with the black cat on it—and set it on the table atop a yellow plastic cloth, and I was glad it had something in it.

I was a neat eater, rarely losing a bite of food I was chewing. This harked back to former days. Based on instinct and experience, food that fell out of my mouth was scarfed up by one of my siblings.

Winston generously augmented my meals with choice treats and tidbits from his plate which were more palatable than the fare in my food bowl.

Dinner was much the same. If there weren't any formal guests, I would join the family for supper. Afterward, I'd hop down and curl up under his chair, my tummy full and my heart content.

I have sampled all kinds of unusual foods that I'm sure most cats never even knew existed. Included were caviar, *pâté de fois gras*, dressed crab, lobster, croissants, pancakes, Yorkshire pudding, beef steak, Maryland chicken, veal escalope, and pork cutlets.

Winston lived large and comfortably, and he taught me how to become a gourmand. I soon regained my fighting weight and only kept from becoming fat and lazy by partaking in a great deal of physical activity.

He also liked to talk to me during lunch. On one occasion he had another guest, but he spoke only to me. I sat on the table completely relaxed, my ears pointed slightly outward.

"Mr. Cat, tell me about your travels and hunting." Then he described some of the best venues to visit in his country realm. He had a keen awareness of every nook and cranny at a place called Chartwell. He was, however, speaking of some paradise I'd never seen.

He also cleaned my eyes with a napkin. He always had an impeccable appearance and dress and wanted me to look my best, too. He hand-fed me morsels of fish.

"It's Dover sole; you'll like it."

I did. He made me the center of attention. I held my head up with my ears alert.

As lunch ended, Winston often rang the bell for an attendant and ordered the cream jug. Then he'd then kindly pour some cream directly on the dining room table for me to lap up. He rarely did this, however, if Clementine were present at lunch.

I observed another eccentric trait: when he or any of his family entered the drawing room, they announced their presence to the others with a "Meow." Were they attempting to be humorous? Or trying to make me feel more comfortable? Either way humans who imitate cats do a poor job of it. It means nothing to us, utter gibberish!

Another human in the household befriended me. Grace, who worked primarily for Clementine, was elegant and kindhearted. I greeted her with a raised tail with its tip bent over as well as with little chirpy purrs of introduction and inquiry. She appeared openhearted, so I rubbed myself against her lower legs. She kept her voice low and non-threatening. Grace reached down and petted me whenever we passed each other.

I came to trust her and would roll over beside her feet, exposing my belly. I actually wanted her to rub me behind my ears, but she would caress my chest instead, which, coming from her, I did not mind.

Chapter 6

A Friend's Tribute

NOT long after I arrived, I heard a voice I didn't recognize. I was curious, and luckily Grace was nearby.

"She's an old friend of Winston's," she explained. "The daughter of former Prime Minister Asquith, her name is Violet Bonham Carter."

My human was extremely fond of her, although she didn't address or pat me.

"Violet, what a pleasure to see you!" He offered a hand and bowed his head.

"Winston, you are looking well," she replied, smiling. "When I first met you a lifetime ago, what impressed me most was your youthful brashness and exuberance. I see some of that enthusiasm in your expression today."

Listening to them, I reclined on my side with my paws extended. My tail was stretched out, not tucked in.

"I couldn't believe my ears," Violet continued, "when you proclaimed, 'We are all worms. But I do believe I am a glowworm.' You certainly lived into that prophecy!

"Furthermore, you saw the world as a blank canvas upon which you painted boldly and in the brightest colors."

"One must always seize the opportunities that present themselves," Winston answered. "Serving as First Lord of the Admiralty in your father's cabinet was one of the finest places for a young politician like me. I relished every opportunity to prepare the Royal Navy for what became the Great War. Despite all that happened subsequently, there was one thing they couldn't take from me—when war came, the fleet was ready!"

"We've shared a long history, and there's something else—a love for the magic, majesty, and power of words," Violet related.

"Words," he agreed, "have always fascinated us, haven't they?"

"Ours has been an intimacy of words as well as of minds."

With that Winston looked deeply at Violet for a long while. They were kindred spirits, and their closeness was palpable. They seemed to be able to communicate without speaking.

The big man's London home was quite large by both human and feline standards. During my first few weeks there, I explored each room where I found an open door. Once I peeked into a darkened room upstairs, and a musty smell assaulted me. I decided to investigate that room at another time.

On another occasion, after Winston fell asleep in his favorite chair in the drawing room, I walked up the stairs and entered a large, airy, cheerful room. There on the sofa sat his wife, Clementine, reserved as usual.

"Good afternoon, Jock," she greeted when she saw me. I looked up into her large, pale, blue-green eyes. White flowers in a vase on the round table by the hearth gave the room a fresh, perfumed scent.

"My, my," she said. "Aren't you a lovely little beast! It's no wonder that Winston is so delighted with you."

Her smiling face with its chiseled nose was topped with white curls. I came over and rubbed my body against her legs. She hesitated then reached down and tickled me briefly behind my ears. I purred, but I got the impression she politely tolerated my presence rather than seeing me as a member of the family the way Winston did.

Morning light streamed through the bay window. I walked over to the wooden shelf that jutted from the window and jumped up. The garden was arrayed below.

A delicate letter opener that lay on the ledge near some envelopes ignited my curiosity. Cupping my paw, I nudged the shiny object. Then I prodded it again.

Clementine's icy, "No!" followed by, "Don't push that on the floor!" startled me. Hunching my shoulders and with my ears down, I slinked out of her room with my tail curled between my legs.

I always kept an eye on Clementine wherever she was in the house because I wanted to stay on her good side.

Each day revealed new delights as I reconnoitered various rooms. The curved staircase took me up and down the four-floor abode. I found the best places to doze, hide, or play. Small knickknacks, a hanging piece of yarn, and other personal mementoes all became objects demanding my immediate scrutiny.

Fortunately, when I couldn't find some human possession to play with, I had my own tail. I'd watch it swaying and grab for it several times with a front paw. Then I'd seriously get into play.

I'd catch it with both paws biting and licking the tip.

Winston's bedroom also had bay windows looking upon the green manicured area beyond. On cold days he might sit there and look through them as if longing to be anywhere but indoors. During good weather, he liked to sit outdoors. Roy would wheel him to a place in the sun where he would bask like a lizard. I would follow and join him. We spent many hours together enjoying the peaceful beauty of his garden.

Opportunely, Winston's house had plenty of tables, chairs, couches, desks, and beds where I could get at eye-level with him. I preferred to be face-to-face with him so our differences in height didn't affect our relative standing. It was only proper that I peer directly into his eyes rather than gawk at the bottom of his legs or ankles.

What I hated most in the house were doors. These prevented me from exercising my liberty. When I wanted to go out, I had to stand by the door until someone noticed me and interpreted my intentions. Similarly, when I was done patrolling my dominion and wanted to come in, I had to wait until someone let me in. Closed doors inside sometimes kept me from getting to my water bowl in my human's bathroom.

After an apparently hectic life of action and drama, the quiet solitude outdoors usually renewed Winston. But one day he coughed more than normal. After wheezing and hacking, he turned to me and said, "Pussycat, it's the worst smog of the year."

Winston was right about the air quality. My sense of smell was much better than his, and the dirty air made it hard for me to breathe too.

The garden was extensive, comprising the entire space behind both townhouses. It was screened by trees, shrubs, and even some flowers, still in bloom despite the coming of winter. A terrace by the house had numerous rock and brick paths throughout it. Short stone walls surrounded flower beds. There I found safe locations where I could take a catnap when it was warm and pleasant. Many of the shrubs were shaped to keep them neat and tidy. Wrought-iron and brick fences added to the security of this sanctuary.

The weather, however, turned cold and misty. As the days passed, it became even colder with dense, freezing fog. Regrettably, there were none of the fragrant bushes that I loved so much. My human's hands had to provide that sensation.

I enjoyed elongating my stride and running at full speed the length of the garden. The fences represented only a temporary barrier. By clawing my way up a tree beside the ivy-covered brick fence, I could range into the neighboring gardens and see the world beyond Winston's.

I found two cats nearby: a female black-and-brown shorthaired tabby with small black vertical stripes between her eyes and a female medium-haired black-and-white tuxedo with a white triangle running from her eyes to her mouth. Among ourselves, felines don't have names, we have smells. Of course, only we can recognize these different smells, which are impossible to describe. Still, we remember all the different cats we have ever met.

When I grew older, I would become the dominant moggy of this clowder. However, this winter they were both older than I was, and I still had many reflexes and interests of a kitten. I was rambunctious, but they tolerated my playfulness and *joie de vivre*.

One garden contained a vicious terrier whom I did my best to avoid. He barked, yipped, and howled whenever he caught my scent. His frightful noise reminded me of the shelter. My hackles rose, and my claws were unsheathed just in case he got through the iron fence that surrounded his home. I planned a hasty strategic withdrawal, since all cats instinctively know th discretion is the better part of valor.

Another tree just beyond the wall allowed me to return to my yard. Occasionally when I was put out at night to answer the call of nature, I'd scale the fence to confer with my feline friends.

Cats don't visit the way humans do. Rather, we share smells and rub alongside each other for comfort. Our soundless presence together is our way of being sociable.

Eventually I became more accustomed to my indoor and outdoor routines. Life was familiar, and that in itself was comforting. On Christmas Day, I was given a special blue collar with an identification disk that read, "Churchill, Hyde Park Gate." My name was not included, but at least I had a place where I knew I belonged.

Chapter 7

Into Battle

ON Boxing Day something white and light fell silently from the sky until there were over three inches of a loose, soft, powdery substance carpeting the ground. I'd seen rain before but never snow. The weather seemed so unpredictable—one day sunny and mild, the next cold and frosty. Nonetheless, I am one fortunate feline—no matter what the weather is, I have somewhere warm and dry to go.

When I sat on the back porch this morning, I gazed warily at the surprising winter landscape. My first steps in snow were tentative as my paws sank through the thin crust. My foot pads felt very cold, then wet, and my ears twitched as a breeze of frosty air caused a shiver to race through my body. I wasn't sure I liked this unexpected sensation.

Cats don't enjoy being wet or cold. Yes, we have a coat of fur, but because the temperature in my human's home was pleasantly warm, my winter coat hadn't grown in. I took small steps forward and soon stood surrounded by snow on every side. It was so cold even the sparrows had disappeared. I sniffed the chilled air. All my favorite scents were gone, replaced by a crisp, icy atmosphere. I certainly didn't feel the call of nature and would have preferred being in the heated house instead.

Snow continued to fall and accumulate. Little did I know that it would remain on the ground almost until spring. Looking through the window in Winston's bedroom I could see the snow-draped garden. I stood on a table with my four feet close together and tail curled around them. Wistfully I looked outside hoping to see something green, but only whites and shades of gray prevailed.

Winston whispered to me, "Ginger, it's been the coldest month since Waterloo."

My ears twitched. The historical reference was unfortunately lost on me.

After overhearing Grace talking with the butler, I found out that Winston had once been a formidable warlord. Now, however, he was more a man who sought peace, both his personal peace and peace for humanity.

I looked for the big man and found him in the drawing room with a man with grayish hair, a rugged face, and bushy eyebrows. They were well into a weighty conversation. Since I didn't hear the introduction when he arrived, the unknown man remained anonymous to me.

Clementine's sofa was unoccupied, but I knew better than to sit there. Instead I chose to curl up on the carpet where the warmth of the fire was comfortable.

The visitor was doing most of the talking while Winston played with the burning logs in the fireplace.

"Eisenhower believed that the H-bomb was no more than just another arrow in the warrior's quiver. Sadly, war's destructive nature has taken a turn toward human extinction, thus making war an anachronism in human affairs," the man said.

Winston nodded, but whether to indicate agreement or simply understanding, I did not know.

"Kennedy seems too inexperienced, taking the world to the brink two months ago. Regrettably, we no longer have the influence to play a major role in world affairs."

Once again Winston bowed his head. As he rolled a log over, it sizzled.

"We need to reclaim our place at the table," the man stated in a confident tone.

Finally Winston spoke. "As I have said before, the price of greatness is responsibility. After the war, the United States stood at the pinnacle of world power.

"First the atomic bomb then the hydrogen weapon carried us into situations which could result in a brutish mutual extermination. Russia also has them, but so far China does not."

Winston stopped again and considered his words. Raising his right hand for emphasis, he said, "To be free from the dread of mass destruction, we must make certain these malignant weapons are our servants and not our masters.

"But the human race has an alternative. It can pursue the swiftest expansion of material well-being that has ever been within reach or even within our dreams."

He paused. Continuing to stoke the blaze, he added, "The population of the English-speaking Commonwealth joined that of the United States. Such cooperation implied strength in the air and on the sea, all over the globe. It included both science and industry. With this moral force, I hoped there would be no quivering, and the balance of power would yield an overwhelming assurance of security."

With that pronouncement Winston stopped speaking and returned to prod his fire. If his guest replied, I didn't hear it. The waves of warmth relaxed me, and I succumbed to sleep.

Because of the cold, wet weather, I chose to spend the least amount of time outdoors as possible. This was certainly going against the grain of any self-respecting cat. We have little rituals, and when we're forced to abandon them, we're apt to react in some other area of our lives. In my case, having to do battle with the elements made me less tolerant of my human's furniture.

I was never one for climbing curtains or scratching couches, chairs, or tables, especially when I had trees. However, with the ground covered in snow, I had to find alternative places to attain some satisfaction.

I found some nice armchairs on the top floor where I could not only sharpen my claws but leave behind some of my scent to mark my territory. My enthusiastic deeds were ultimately revealed. Winston was understanding, a quality he extended to me but to few others, but Clementine was irate.

Whenever I saw her, I hunched my shoulders and put my ears down. I didn't feel contrite, however, because I was just being a cat. Nonetheless, she didn't bend down to pet me for a while. Happily for me, Winston compensated for her lack of acceptance with extra food treats.

The cold weather prevented me from getting sufficient daily exercise. To use up my excess energy and settle into a nice nap, I liked to run around at full tilt on silent feet. I would tear around the house with frenetic speed, sometimes landing on couches with my claws unsheathed. The cushions weren't too worse for wear, however.

Without adequate exercise, my immunity suffered. Not surprisingly, I was off my game for a few days with an upset tummy. I felt listless and eager to hide again. However, a week's worth of terribly tasting medication from the vet cured my affliction.

Fortunately, when the middle of winter arrived, so had my thick, warm coat, and just in time. Late one night I heard a commotion. I had been resting peacefully on a chair outside my human's bedroom.

The night nurse informed the butler, "The power's gone out."

After checking the fuse box, the butler reported to Clementine, "The main fuse blew in Sir Winston's half of the house, ma'am."

She became alarmed and said, "We can't let my husband sleep in an unheated room! We'd better move him before he freezes!"

It didn't feel too cool to me, because of my fur. Humans aren't as well-endowed as cats are.

Winston took all this in stride. "I'll be fine with some extra blankets. Just let me get back to bed." He's really keen about his rest and hates for it to be disturbed.

The butler, driver, and male nurse paid no attention to his orders. Instead they disassembled Winston's heavy, wooden bed and moved it to the reception room of the townhouse next door which still had power. The big man was distressed and almost convinced the men to transfer his bed back to his bedroom. Raising her voice in a high pitch, Clementine settled the matter.

"Winston, you're sleeping over in #28 tonight. That's final!"

He did not like changes like this. Accordingly, he woke the next morning two hours earlier than usual. With a huff he dressed. Instead of having his breakfast in bed and reading the newspapers, he crept into the nearby drawing room. There he sulked until the electrician came by, fixed the blown fuse, and restored the power to his bedroom. Finally, his bed was disassembled, carried over to its original location, and reassembled to his obvious satisfaction.

I had been unconscionably ignored throughout this little drama. I'm sure I earned a nice morsel for breakfast by being calm during the entire calamity. I edged next to my human and rubbed against his leg.

He looked at me, removed the cigar from his lips, and in a mischievous tone said, "Mr. Cat, let's eat!"

Chapter 8

These Are Great Days

I lay under the big man's chair during an informal supper in the dining room with Winston, Clementine, and me. The housemaid had taken away the dessert dishes and Stilton cheese that I've grown to like.

Winston played with his unlit cigar. Pushing his coffee cup aside, he smiled at Clementine. "Was there a reason you had one of my favorite wartime meals tonight? Irish stew just the way I like it, with plenty of small onions and not much broth?" he asked.

I think it will be one of my favorites as well. The lamb was tender and moist, and I lapped up every drop of stock I was given.

"I knew you would notice. Before D-Day, your Tuesday luncheons with General Eisenhower always got off to a good start with Irish stew. Then, like now, you were under a great deal of stress," she observed.

Winston was quiet as he considered how to reply. Then groping for the precise word, he exclaimed, "Clemmie, the world has passed me by.

All the things I cherish most seem to be slipping away. I can no longer make a difference in... in..."

He became exasperated when he couldn't express his thoughts the way he intended. With his rising voice, my tail swayed into motion.

"My darling," Clemmie said tenderly, with a smile on her face and a softness in her eyes, "everything is all right. Your legacy is solid and immutable. Your efforts, and yours alone, gave this nation and the world the way out of the misery and chaos of a world at war. That achievement will always be yours."

Winston listened thoughtfully as he took in her words. "I have profound misgivings about the future," he continued. "Our leaders are more concerned with appearance than substance. Grave dangers lie before us. Who will be the voice in the wilderness now?"

"My dearest love, everyone knows you were the beacon of truth and hope before Hitler plunged the world into war. And it was you who stood firm and steadfast when Halifax attempted to get the Cabinet to negotiate with that madman."

Winston nodded. "That holy fox," he muttered. "Those were stirring times. But now they're relegated to history books, as am I."

"Pug, do you remember that awful day in late 1940 when the bombers dropped incendiaries on the City?"

A hush surrounded Winston. In his mind he must have been relieving those terrible events. "It was Sunday, December 29th, the 114th day of the Blitz," he informed. "How could I ever forget it?"

Grace had previously mentioned that Winston's mind was photographic as well as encyclopedic. His recall was extraordinary!

"Scores, nay, hundreds of German bombers, Heinkels, Junkers, and Dorniers departed their airfields in France and dropped well over ten thousand firebombs on London. My orders were that St. Paul must be saved at all costs.

"First, I heard the wailing sirens—then the sound of engines—followed by the gentler sound of the falling incendiaries, like a whoosh, compared to the screams of the high explosive ones as they plummeted into shops and buildings.

"My heart ached at the loss of life which was in the thousands and the destruction of structures so treasured to our race. Guildhall and eight Christopher Wren churches were consumed by the infernos. Railway stations on docks on both sides of the river were not spared. We had well over seven hundred blazes, of which ten were major."

His words were mesmerizing. My ears listened to the pain that emanated from my human's remembrance.

Clementine took up the story. "And the next day you toured the damage. I was at your side as we stepped uneasily over rubble. Many of the fires were still smoldering, baking our faces in their evil warmth and scorching our throats with their caustic smoke.

"As we walked amongst the ruins, Londoners, many of whom had lost everything, came out to cheer you. Your presence, like the dome of St. Paul's, gave them confidence and hope.

"Winston, as we walked together, your face was grim yet resolute. I knew inside your anger seethed like the fires that burned deep within the City. I reached over and squeezed your hand, like I'm doing now."

Her hand reached across the table and clasped his.

"I knew this monstrous act would be repaid in full on those evil men. But at that moment I felt it necessary to comfort you from the hurts that shook your soul.

"Then, like now, you have nothing to fear, my dearest own Winston. I'm beside you for the duration. As you said, 'Let us go forward together.'"

Tears glistened in Winston's eyes as emotions enveloped him. His chest heaved, and he exhaled a great breath. He then collected himself. "Darling Kat, like I said then, 'Keep buggering on.' It's still applicable, isn't it? KBO!"

Clementine threw her head back and gave her infectious, deep-throated cackling laugh. Winston chuckled and slapped his knee.

"How about a game of bezique, my darling one?" Winston asked.

I had just witnessed the invincible bond that connected these two remarkable humans.

Chapter 9

The End of the Beginning

WINSTON was gone. According to a housemaid, he went somewhere called Monte Carlo for two weeks, a length of time that meant nothing to me, to stake his money on red. Since he left, I have been blue. No one spoils me the way he does.

It rained the day he departed, but my human was in good spirits. I heard his staff congratulating him about being made an honorary citizen of the United States. Grace told me his American mother would have been proud of him. I had sat on Winston's lap while he watched the special television program from America the night before but didn't understand what was taking place.

Clementine did not accompany him but instead stayed with Mary and her family over a holiday called Easter.

Days passed without Winston. I wandered all over the house looking for him but to no avail. He wasn't even using his bed. I began napping in the drawing room as he spent most of his waking hours in that room, but he still didn't appear. I was on my own and longed for us to be together.

One of the housemaids took care of me, feeding me or letting me out. There were, however, no games with the newspapers and no special treats. Furthermore, I missed my human's visitors. When they were here, I learned more about him.

The yard had erupted with flowers and spring greenery. The afternoons were warm and sunny. I found my favorite wall and took a nap.

Cats dream in color. Sometimes I am hunting food in dense green woods. On other occasions I'm communing with felines whom I've known, like my siblings.

My reveries are mostly happy, pleasant times. I once even dreamed I was being fed by my human on his bed. When I woke, I headed to his room, hoping it was real and not a product of my imagination while asleep, but he was not present. If I've had any nightmares, I don't recall them.

I discovered that Winston's townhouses had a lush, spacious garden on one side and a hard, gray ground populated by what humans called cars on the other. All my travels over the fences had never led me to this other artificial domain.

Being a cat in a human world means that we often do not understand what is happening.

For example, one day a housemaid caught me and carried me out the front door to the street side of the house. I didn't like being grabbed and tried to evade her. I wondered whether Winston had ever been captured and had to escape.

The housemaid carried my squirming body to a waiting car and put me on the back seat. She did not accompany me. After she closed the door, the driver sitting in the front seat started the car, which made loud mechanical sounds. Then it was in motion. He had his hands on the wheel but otherwise sat still. These contraptions move much faster than I can run and are noisy and smelly, too.

I was vaguely reminded of the stressful occasion when I was taken in a box on a similar journey before I met my human. A wave of panic caused my hackles to rise. My body tensed in readiness. Had I done something wrong? Did I spoil my welcome by clawing the armchairs too aggressively? Were they returning me to the shelter with its small cage, poor food, and howling dogs? This time, however, I was not in a box and could see through the windows as houses, trees, and other cars passed by.

As the number of cars increased, our movement slowed, and the noise increased. I put my front paws against the door and felt the vibrations. When the right opportunity occurred, perhaps I could jump out and run to safety.

Our car soon stopped and waited in a long line of other cars. There were loud blasts of sound all around. Huge, noisy birds called airplanes were hurtling across the sky.

After a considerable wait, the driver exited but closed his door before I could scramble through it. He stood at attention at the door on the other side of my seat. I readied my body for flight in case the opportunity presented itself.

Suddenly the door opened. Just as I was about to leap from the car, Winston's bulky form slid gently onto the seat next to me!

"Mr. Cat, so good to see you! I'm glad to be back," he cried.

I was so excited to see my human! I jumped into his lap and rubbed one side of my forehead and then the other on his smiling face.

There is such a thing as a properly executed head nudge. I begin at the top of my head and roll my head to the front of my right ear rubbing along his face. Then I return to the top of my head and rub him to the front of my left ear. I alternate this until I have exhausted my spurt of enthusiasm and ensured I have reclaimed him with my scent.

I also held my tail high, but it rolled into graceful large curls with the tip forming a question mark. In addition, I was purring with delight.

I must have let my claws involuntarily extend because they caught in his waistcoat. He didn't mind; he simply repositioned my body, still allowing me to stand on him. I commenced pushing my front paws into his belly, kneading him left, right, left, right, all the while lavishing him with whimpers of joy and head bumps. I can't imagine he ever had such a warm homecoming!

Winston responded by rubbing me from my head to my tail. Then I felt his face pressed into the side of my neck. I heard him whispering, "I missed you, too."

After the luggage was loaded into the trunk, the Sergeant, Winston's trusty, balding bodyguard with the neatly trimmed mustache, got in the passenger's seat in the front, and the other human reassumed his position behind the steering wheel. In a respectful voice he asked, "Chartwell, sir?"

The big man replied, "Yes, Chartwell, and make it quick! Hurry, hurry!"

Why do humans always say things more than once? And Winston, it seems, was always in a rush.

I had survived my first separation from Winston, but this occasion signified a transformation. He was genuinely delighted to see me. Humans can grow very close to their cats. We certainly have room to grow even closer, but as I later realized, such familiarity requires sharing more life-changing events.

Winston was upbeat and sang to himself several verses of "Abdulla Bulbul Ameer," a music-hall ditty popular in Victorian England.

> "There are heroes in plenty, and well
> known to fame
> In the ranks that were led by the Czar,
> But the bravest of all was a man by the
> name
> Of Ivan Potschjinski Skidar.
> He could imitate Toole, play Euchre and
> Pool
> And perform on the Spanish guitar.
> In fact quite the cream of the Muscovite
> team
> Was Ivan Potschjinski Skidar."

Without a care in the world, he amused himself with the song while the Sergeant, looking over his right shoulder, smiled.

Little did I know that just as I was beginning to feel confident in my surroundings, yet another surprise awaited me.

Chapter 10

The New World

AFTER leaving the airport and threading our way through the city, the car followed narrow tree-lined roads into the country. The spring greens of foliage were sometimes punctuated by vibrant grass fields. The world was reborn in leafy hues of life.

I sat on the seat next to my human and purred contentedly. The car entered an open gate and a large, rather ordinary-looking red brick country manor of several stories loomed ahead. Unlike the row upon row of townhouses that occupied the cul-de-sac of his London home, this house stood by itself.

Winston, looking like a proud father, proclaimed, "Ah, Chartwell!" He gestured grandly at his house and continued, "We shape our buildings and afterwards our buildings shape us." It was hard to miss the excitement in his voice and the vigor in his face. Clearly this place meant a great deal to him.

A man stepped forward and opened the car door to welcome him home. I then jumped from my seat to the ground and stood watching the arrival ritual. Housemaids, nurses, butlers, cooks, and gardeners all lined up in front of the wooden double front doors. A valet opened the large trunk of the car and extracted over a dozen pieces of luggage.

Some say a human's life is defined by his surroundings. If so, Chartwell was a perfect reflection of Winston's expansive and ebullient personality. The gardens, lakes, ponds, walls, and other buildings all grew out of his many interests and hobbies, with fields and forests surrounding them.

Chartwell stood like a novel among a bookcase of non-fiction works, a refuge from the stresses of what had once been a demanding public life. It was symbolic of existence itself—a fish in water, a bird in air, Winston Churchill at Chartwell.

Like his London home, his country abode was large and would take a while to explore. But that would have to wait. Winston was eager to walk across the terrace lawn and survey his realm, and I wanted to be with him.

On the other side of the property, his house transformed into a charming garden or lake front that included bay windows, stepped gables, imposing fireplaces, and multiple wings. Walking with his cane, he slowly neared a low brick wall. Standing beside him, I beheld a sea of verdant hues beneath a pale blue sky.

"Just look at this majestic view, Pussycat!" he exclaimed, puffing on his cigar. "The Weald of Kent—there is no finer view in all England."

I'm not as influenced by scenic beauty. I am more curious about what tasty creatures lived among the bushes and trees. I noticed that beeches, oaks, limes, elms, chestnuts, and maples could be found in Winston's woodlands. I stopped to sniff the hanging sprays of sweet-scented wisteria. They offered a great location to hide and wait for nearby birds.

Winston went inside to take a nap, the travel having totally exhausted him. Being left on my own, I began an inspection of Chartwell, starting on the ground floor where attendants were still carrying luggage in from the car. I found Clementine's bedroom supplied with vases of white flowers. There were many new intriguing scents to explore.

On the other side of the hall was the library, and farther down the hall, the still larger drawing room. So far, all the rooms were bigger and airier, as well as more lavish and opulent, than the corresponding rooms in London. I jumped up on the rust-colored sofa and decided it would enable superb catnaps.

Where did Winston go? I followed the scent of his cigar upstairs, past the dining room where some housemaids were setting the dinner table. I hope they brought my cat bowl, too. The cigar smell was strong down the hall, and at the end was Winston's study. Open beam rafters, tall, tome-filled bookcases, large paintings, banners hanging from the ceiling—so much to see! The study had a solid, staunch feel to it. I would have to try the sofas and desks to find the nicest place to perch.

I padded across the Persian rug into the open door to the right of the hearth. There he was—fast asleep in bed, so I hopped up beside him. I too was fatigued, from both the hectic car trip and the excitement of being reunited with him.

The daily routine at Winston's country home was essentially the same as at the London home. He woke late and had breakfast in bed while he read the newspapers. I hopped onto his bed and purred while he stroked me from head to tail, but my presence did not distract him from his pattern of doing things, which included sharing tasty tidbits with me from whatever he was eating.

I noticed Winston was right-handed when it came to writing or flashing his V-for-victory. He used either hand, however, to hold his cigar, grasp his brandy snifter, or caress me. The Sergeant, who also dabbled in oils, once said Winston painted with his right hand.

When he was at Chartwell, so was Grace. She seemed to run the operations of this large country house. Yes, she took instructions from Clementine, but she was the go-to person. The name Grace aptly described her, too, as she was always graciously kind to me. Little did I know that I would spend a major portion of my life at Chartwell with her!

My human's bedroom was small and cozy. It was tucked in next to his study. I liked to lie either on the Persian rug or on the comfy white flower-patterned armchair at the foot of his bed. He had a bay window that offered a magnificent view of his kingdom.

He always took a late afternoon nap to rejuvenate him for his evening activities. He donned a silk vest-like outfit that left his pink body naked below the waist and a sleep mask or as he called it, "my eye blinkers." He slid between soft bedsheets that pampered his very sensitive skin.

I hid under his bed until Roy, who assisted in undressing him, had left. Then I vaulted up by his feet where I drifted off next to my snoring human.

I was less successful in the evenings. When Winston put his book aside and settled down to rest, I positioned myself between his legs, as he liked to recline on his back with his feet wide apart. Occasionally he wiggled his toes or kicked at me with his feet to get me to move, but I didn't like being disturbed from a deep nap and usually reacted by biting his toes.

Invariably Roy tried to shoo me off the bed, claiming the big man needed his sleep. I swished my tail more quickly to show my displeasure. But he persisted. When he did this, Winston would say, "Nonsense! Yellow Cat stays."

Eventually Roy had his way. He knew that Winston always managed to fall fast asleep right away, so I was invited to leave when the lights were turned off. A curtain was slid across the archway which separated the bedroom from the study.

I then scrambled up on a plush cream-colored armchair by the fireside. I remained there with the night nurse throughout the evening, frequently channeling my nocturnal energies by trying to catch the bats which flew among the high rafters. Jumping on either the cluttered stand-up desk or his sit-down desk allowed me to get closer to the flapping nuisances.

More often than not, I knocked onto the floor pens, paperweights, or Winston's klopper, his hole puncher. The small lamp that illuminated the study cast an eerie light made more sinister by the swooping winged mammals. This unnerved the women who had the duty each night. I was delighted to be their knight in shining armor and protect them.

Chapter 11

The True Glory

MY internal alarm clock caused me to wake early. During the dimness of a misty dawn, and again at sunset, when my vision was at its best, I reconnoitered the lake side of the house, crossing the lawn and advancing to the old kitchen garden. The tall grasses brushed like soft whispers against my legs. Once I departed the threshold of Winston's house, I automatically switched my mindset from well-behaved house pet to predator cat. All my senses, strength, and reflexes were directed to my survival.

Frequently I added a midday sojourn because I was always curious about who had been in my area. Yes, mine—as Winston claimed the home, I likewise claimed the grounds outside. I rarely went more than a few hundred yards from the house. The head gardener claimed there were well over eighty acres at Chartwell, but initially I only scratched the surface, no pun intended, of places I visited.

I had a ritual that involved patrolling my domain to sample the smells. When I wanted to investigate each new smell, I first gave it a good sniff. This might yield who had visited, its age, gender, or even what food it recently consumed. Then I opened my mouth, grimaced, and deeply inhaled the scent to get a better taste of it. That would be my first indication of predators, such as other cats, or better still, of food. So far, I haven't detected any other felines. Claw marks on tree trunks are another sign of cats marking their territory, and only mine were present.

I frequently found a high perch atop the stone wall that divided the terrace lawn and the orchard. Here I could survey the area below for intruders or supplemental meals. Being in the larger, lower branches of the crotch of a tree, such as the mulberry near the kitchen garden, was another good vantage place to check my territory.

I quickly developed a detailed and accurate mental map of my patch. I rechecked scents and occasionally reinforced my earlier ones. I marked my realm by rubbing my chin, cheek, flank, or tail against strategic objects—rocks, bushes, stalks, or plants. Being a male, I might also spray a warning to potential competitors. However, I didn't try this inside, as I had previously incurred the ire of the big man's wife.

I had to understand what was happening in my territory so that I could locate food there or defend myself from intruders. Equally important was finding a cozy place where I could safely take a catnap when the sleep chemicals in my body took control. My internal map allowed me to devise several paths across my land, in case a special escape route was needed to evade a prowling predator.

I don't need much space to squeeze through an opening or densely packed vegetation. My vibs (vibrissae or whiskers for you humans) let me gauge the gap so my body doesn't get stuck. I can also detect small air currents that can bend my vibs and in effect help me "see" my way in the dark. These tell me whether my head and shoulders can get through a small opening. If they can, the rest of my body will make it.

There were foxes, hawks, and owls who'd represent a threat if I let my guard down. Humans were potential predators, too, although most of the dozen or fewer who worked on the estate were congenial, or they would have incurred Winston's wrath.

Chartwell was lush with trees, shrubs, and a profusion of flowers. In spring there were daffodils, tulips, anemones, and hyacinths. As summer neared, iris, gladioli, Canterbury Bells, and Sweet Williams bloomed. Roses of every color appeared, from the perfumed deep red ones to the delicate yet almost scentless white ones. I liked the cheerful, wild daisies that grew beneath the terrace lawn wall. Dahlias emerged in fall, followed by chrysanthemums and fuchsias. I came to love to nibble on the sweet peas just before we would leave for the London home for winter.

I can see colors but evidently not with the same vibrant, saturated hues that humans can. I can see much better in the dark and need only a fraction of the light that humans require. My eyes are optimized for hunting; hence, my peripheral vision is slighter greater, and my acuity lets me see a fast-moving mouse within a pounce or two's distance. One deficiency I was not aware of, and subsequently received a rude awakening from, was that some slow-moving objects look stationary to cats.

I also staked out my territory inside Winston's abode. I chinned all his furniture, especially his bed, prominent objects on his desk, and of course, the big man himself. This I did every morning on meeting him at breakfast as well as throughout the day. He was mine, all mine, and I claimed him. Fortunately, there were no other felines or even a foul dog I had to share him with.

Every moment at Chartwell resembled bright light radiating from the facets of a diamond. This cherished place was a glory personified. Not only was it a feast for the eyes but it also possessed special uplifting powers. Here Winston was at peace.

Chapter 12

One Great Family

As I explored my human's realm, I often discovered a room that had previously been closed to me, such as the furnace room. It contained the main house boilers and additionally was where they stored the dahlias during the winter months.

I had been on the garden side near the house where an open door and a smoky scent aroused my curiosity. The walls were crusted with creosote, and the boiler fronts were cold, having not been used lately. The entire room was solidly built, and as I found out, was constructed to function also as a bomb shelter, one of several at Chartwell.

Since one of the younger gardener's assistants, working inside, didn't mind my presence, I lay down and watched while he stacked some tools against a wall. My neck itched under my collar, and I lifted my leg quickly and scratched the offending feeling.

I must have dozed because I heard the door to the furnace room slam shut. In the dark I jumped to my feet. Walking to the door, I found it was closed, tightly closed. With my paw, I pushed it, but it did not move.

Suddenly the door flew open, and daylight streamed in. The young man stood there gaping at me.

"There you are!" he exclaimed. "Almost forgot you were in here. Good thing I remembered. We don't use the furnace room during the warmer months. You might have been trapped in here for weeks!"

With my head held high, I walked out into the sunshine as if nothing had happened.

The big man's family often visited. His youngest daughter, Mary, must have lived nearby because she came frequently. She was kind to me from the day I arrived at Winston's London home, and I could always count on her to bend down and pat my head. It's possible she enjoys all animals, but more likely she just adores me. She was cheerful, courteous, and no doubt the pick of the litter.

"Jock, you're such a welcome addition here. Papa simply loves you," she volunteered.

People tend to open up when they're with me. It's because I never interrupt them. I rubbed against her legs and purred.

Winston's son, Randolph, on the other hand, was a most unlikable man. He frequently shouted, the spontaneous combustion of his volatile personality. He was arrogant as well as pushy and had an ongoing, stormy quarrel with his father. There was an unusual love-hate relationship going on between them.

I disliked the sharp tone of his voice, a noise that was upsetting to my ears. When he first saw me, it was in the evening, and I whined when I heard his loud voice.

"I'm sure we can work this out, Chumbolly," Winston said earnestly.

"I've always hated that nickname. I'm not the Chumbolly any more, Papa!"

"Indeed, you're not," sighed Winston.

I simply don't like it when humans argue. Intense noises torture me, and I have to respond.

The son bellowed, "Papa, you must get rid of that awful cat. I can't stand that howling he's making!"

Randolph roughly shooed me away with his foot. I scooted under a nearby chair but not before seeing dog pee on his pants cuffs. Yes, seeing it as well as smelling it, because it fluoresced in the darkened room. Felines have exceptional powers of eyesight that also allow us to see potential food at night by the glowing liquid trails rodents leave in the grass.

I watched him warily. I always maintained a very low profile around him yet kept my claws at the ready just in case. I groomed myself more when he was around. That's one of my stress relieving strategies.

I later met Winston's bubbly, red-haired middle daughter, Sarah. She was said to possess an artistic spirit. Perhaps she inherited this from her father. We had little interaction.

The big man also had another daughter, his firstborn, Diana. She rarely visited and seemed aloof when she did. She must have carried some difficult burdens of life with her, but Winston and Clementine seemed to think she had turned the corner and was doing better.

Because Winston's hands shook and he didn't have the power to concentrate intensely, he no longer painted, leaving his favorite pastime as a thing of the past. Perhaps he painted in his mind as he sat and surveyed the beautiful vistas here. Many of his earlier landscapes hung on the walls in his studio. I'm not a good judge of art, but he must have loved nature considering the number of trees and field scenes remembered in oils.

Frankly, I have no creative talent or interests. Hunting is the art form at which I excel. Squirrels, moles, mice, and birds were my masterpieces. I have to admit I'm a pretty good mouser. I know that proper distance is the key. I have to be close to my prey before the final lunge.

My mother had taught my siblings and me how to hunt, first by bringing the catch home to us to eat. That got us used to the exotic new tastes. When we got older, we accompanied her and watched as she stalked a small rat or bird. Cats never hunt in packs; we were there to learn the proper way to do it.

Her advance was stealthy and silent. The only indication she was about to pounce was the small, almost imperceptible twitch of her tail immediately before she jumped at the prey. Mother also taught us to be patient, which can make the difference between having a full tummy or an empty one.

Our first efforts were clumsy, and the intended victim flew or bolted beyond our reach before we arrived. Eventually, we were able to snatch slower creatures and were rewarded with a little something extra to eat. We might have gone hungry, however, had not the woman who lived nearby continued to feed us scraps.

Birds are more a challenge to catch than small rodents. In order to grasp birds, I needed to hide in the brush and wait for them to land nearby. Otherwise they were likely to evade me. Upwind attacks are always a must. Fortunately, I have excellent eye-paw coordination, and my success rate has been more meals than fasts.

My marmalade tabby pattern helps to camouflage me. Surprisingly, these markings let me resemble a snake, so when I'm curled up, a hawk or owl thinks twice before swooping down to attack. I snooze better knowing this.

Once the gardener mentioned to me that poisonous adders occasionally frequented the grounds around Chartwell. If I ever encounter one, I'll give it a wide berth.

I studied Winston's golden orfe in their special ponds, but they looked almost half as long as I was, much too big to grab, although they moved slowly enough. They also appeared closer than they really were. When I put my paw into the glass-like surface, it got wet. In surprise, I jumped back from the pond's edge.

Late one afternoon, the big man was sitting under the shadow of the great cedar that stood below the terrace lawn. His large, ten-gallon cowboy hat, so appropriate because of his American heritage, shaded his face, and a rug that encased his frail body warmed him. I lay on his chest with my vibs close to his chin.

"Mr. Cat, you're tickling me," he teased. I reached out with my right paw casually touching his ear. He laughed and extended his hand to rub the top of my head. Instead I licked his fingers and nibbled on them lightly.

Feeling ebullient, Winston broke into what Grace explained was a song about imperial exaltation which Winston had sung as a young soldier.

> "It's the soldiers of the Queen, my lads
> Who've been the lads, who've seen the lads,
> In the fight for England's glory, lads,
> Of her world-wide glory let us sing."

His voice was light and carried the tune well.

On occasion I missed lunch with Winston. When he noticed my absence from the table, one of the housemaids or nurses was commissioned to locate me and bring me to him. Sometimes I chose to remain out of sight. He'd then ask, "What happened to the yellow cat?" If they couldn't find me, lunch would begin without me. Afterward he'd tell me what special treats I would have enjoyed.

On one occasion instead of tracing my familiar path through the garden side of the house, I chose to investigate the front of the house. A long straight stretch of roadway extends outward from the parking area and gate in front of the house.

I was standing in the road with the sun at my back. I did not hear a car slowly approaching from behind me. When I detected its sound, I turned but was looking directly into the sun. I finally saw the car, but it was not moving, or so I thought. The next thing I knew, it smacked me forcefully, and the world turned black.

Chapter 13

The Dream

A complete and total darkness surrounded me. I couldn't see anything even with my light sensitive eyes. Instantly my heart pounded in my chest, and my fur stood on end. My claws readied to confront any unknown danger. I was poised to leap to safety once I could determine the best direction to retreat. My pupils completely dilated as I struggled to see.

A shaft of lightning suddenly illuminated my view. I could see that I was standing at the precipice of a tall ravine. Where was I? What was I doing here? A distant rumble of thunder echoed in the distance.

Then the rain fell. At first it was only a drizzle, but with each passing instant, it became heavier. Soon it was coming down harder than I had ever felt it. The drops splashed over the muddy ground and bounced up on my underside. I quickly became a soggy sack of fur that shivered more from worry than being chilled to the bone.

Cats don't like water. It doesn't have the cleansing power that humans seem to appreciate. I remember padding into the small bathroom next to my human's bedroom. The sliding door was open. He was cavorting in the sunken tube like an excited marine creature, his body a bright pink from the temperature of the water. He splashed warm water all over the floor. Some even grazed my tail and back, and I instantly scampered out of range.

Any self-respecting cat will tell you this pithy truth: have tongue, can lick. That sums up the essence of our cleanliness. If I can't reach it, it doesn't need to be cleaned. Thus, any more moisture than a tongue-full is wasted on us.

Another flash of lightning and a more rapid report of thunder told me the storm was moving closer. I felt the ground beneath my paws become sodden in the rain, crumbling away into a moving ooze.

Then a bolt of lightning erupted so brightly that my pupils instantly constricted. It cast a brief but eerie brilliance on the land around me. As the blackness returned, I could see in my mind's eye the mucky ground with a deluge pelting down with the force of a tall waterfall.

At my feet the ground sloped away sharply into a ravine. And then the almost instantaneous clap of thunder thrust me into motion. The ground deserted my paws as I flew into the turbulent air.

I landed on my feet, of course, as cats always do. We have a natural righting reflex aided by the conservation of angular momentum.

My paws touched the muddy slope, but I was carried downward by the steepness of the incline. I toppled over, and tucking my head in, careened first onto my shoulder then my back, head over heels, faster and faster, toward the bottom of the ravine. I was completely out of control, and I sensed that I might not survive this ordeal.

Chapter 14

The Unrelenting Struggle

IN a groggy haze I could hear sounds floating over me. My eyes were sealed shut. My entire body ached as I lay on my side, and my breaths came with waves of pain. My head hurt as well. I recognized Winston's voice.

"What happened?" he asked.

Another replied. "A young lad on a bicycle found him on the side of the road. It looks like he was hit by a passing car. He picked him up and carried him to the head gardener's cottage. We got to you as quickly as we could."

I heard Roy say, "Sir Winston, you can't let him suffer. Perhaps it's best to put him out of his misery."

Someone placed his ear over my chest. I could smell my human. He sounded like he was sobbing. His voice was so distraught that his words were barely audible.

"He's still very much alive. As long as I have the final say, he'll not be put down."

Another surge of agony swept over me. I tried to move my front leg, but the effort was too great. My world dissolved into blackness.

My eyes opened, and I was lying on a table in a strange, brightly lit room with an unusual chemical smell. A man in a white coat was looking at me closely while off to the side I saw Grace with worry etched across her gentle face.

"Doctor, what do you think? Will he pull through?" Grace asked. "Winston's terribly worried. He said to spare no expense."

"In my years as a vet, I've seen quite a few cats who were hit by a car. Most were run over by the wheels, and I could do nothing to save them. Mercifully, this cat must have been struck a glancing blow that shoved him to the side of the road. His jaw is clearly broken, and he's suffered other abrasions and trauma. I'll wire up his jaw. If he survives the next forty-eight hours, he might have a fighting chance. But cats are tricky creatures. Just not eating for two days can render his survival tenuous."

"But you'll do everything possible?" Grace inquired.

"I'll do my best. Whether he pulls through is probably in someone else's hands."

"I'll report this to Winston. I know he'll want to stop by and check on him. He lost his first poodle, Rufus, when he was run over by a bus in Brighton. He's extremely fond of this cat."

"Tell him to give us about seventy-two hours. If Jock is still with us, he can come by then," the veterinarian replied.

I slept and slept. My jaw ached, and I felt raw wherever my body rested against the small cage I was in. Lying on a towel didn't provide very much cushioning. Incidentally, the cage made me feel safer since I couldn't defend myself. But I was too sore even to think about food.

The vet and his nurse walked by.

"He's awake, doctor," she offered.

"So he is! Let's have a look at him."

The vet opened the front of the cage. He then took an odd-looking device that hung around his neck and put one end into his ears and the other to my body. He listened for a short while.

"I can hear crackles and whistling in his lungs. I think that confirms it. He's caught bacterial pneumonia. That's consistent with the fever, difficulty breathing, lack of appetite, and sluggishness we're seeing. We'll confirm this with a blood test and a chest x-ray. I think we'll skip a tracheal wash for now as that might be too invasive and upsetting. Let's keep him on fluids to prevent dehydration. We'll start him on penicillin, too."

"Your prognosis, doctor?"

"I'm optimistic, assuming we can eradicate this disease early enough with the antibiotics. But time will tell."

In the brief moments I was conscious, I caught a glimpse of the vet and his nurse stopping by my cage as well as the others in his treatment room. Once I thought I saw Grace peering at me. It was hard to tell whether I was really awake or just dreaming. Gradually the throbbing in my jaw and body subsided. I was still a young cat, and youthfulness tends to aid in faster recovery, or so I've been told.

When I opened my eyes next, I was home! I was resting on a towel atop a comfortable cushion inside a small wicker basket. An audience of familiar faces hovered over me—Winston, Grace, Roy, even Clementine.

Winston leaned toward me. Tears misted from his anxious eyes. His lips quivered, and his voice wavered as he gently spoke to me.

"Oh, Jock. You gave us such a scare. I don't know what I'd do if I lost you."

He called me, Jock. Winston called me, Jock! I must be more essential to him now.

He then gave a forced smile and ever so gently rubbed my back. Of course, I could smell his hand lotion with its enticing lavender scent. I sighed. I felt happy to be among those who loved me.

"Jock, I, too, was once struck by an automobile—when I exited a taxi in New York in 1931," Winston related. "I forgot about cars driving on the right side of the road and looked in the wrong direction for oncoming traffic. I was quite banged up for a while."

He understood my experience. I tried to purr to let him know how much I appreciated him.

Winston paused then added, "KBO, Jock. KBO!"

Then my human, holding a small saucer filled with cream, dipped a finger into it and placed it near my mouth. My small pink tongue darted out and licked the cream off his finger. We repeated this action until my shrunken tummy couldn't take any more. I looked up into Winston's tearful eyes and held his gaze for a moment. At that instant a special bond formed that linked our lives forever.

Chapter 15

All Will Be Well

GOOD country living transformed me from an invalid into a strong, robust cat. It took a while, but I welcomed each new day with a sense of adventure. Both Winston and I lived very simply—as he observed, "with all the essentials of a life well understood and provided for." For him it was, "hot baths, cold champagne, new peas, and old brandy." For me it was sumptuous meals, long naps, affable companionship, and energizing venues to roam and hunt. My tastes, however, are modest: I am easily satisfied with the best.

Living at Chartwell was special! Every day was a holiday and every meal a banquet, particularly since my accident.

I overheard one of the secretaries telling Winston that he had received a letter from an American university who wanted to bestow on him another honorary degree.

He seemed especially talkative today. He nodded and without batting an eye casually informed her, "Perhaps no one ever passed so few examinations and received so many degrees!"

Cats have no need for these human rituals. They're beneath us. I derive ample satisfaction from catching a mouse and don't need an applauding audience to congratulate me. A tasty delight is sufficient!

Winston had the habit of doing what he wanted when he wanted to do it, just like me! Clementine, Grace, Roy, and others were, however, accustomed to the big man's unpunctual ways. Meals began when he arrived. Although there were preferences when lunch or dinner were scheduled to begin, these were simply suggestions to him. Excursions via car started whenever he moved to the front door regardless of when the events were to commence.

Clementine once described how her husband had always been late for trains. "Winston is a sporting man. He likes to give the train a chance to get away."

Winston definitely had his own priorities and sense of time, or lack of it. This was perfectly fine with me because a feline appreciates an independent streak.

Spring rains and cooler temperatures caused the trees and shrubs to explode with delicate hues of green. Part of my rehabilitation was to range farther than usual from the large country home. I explored the small ponds he created. His golden orfe danced under the water in a swirl of colors: reds, oranges, browns, and white. I still wondered how they tasted.

I surveyed Winston's roses and circled back along the stone walkway under a vine-covered pergola that was supported by columns which fronted the Marlborough Pavilion, an open room honoring his great ancestor. The other side of the brick wall was edged by colorful roses climbing up the wall. I then walked down the steps and proceeded along the base of the hedge that followed the terrace lawn above.

I also padded in the other direction, trotting across and down from the terrace lawn. Then I'd arch up against an apple or pear tree in his orchard and strop my claws.

My human's kitchen garden possessed tantalizing smells, and each one needed to be fully investigated. It provided an endless supply of fresh vegetables and herbs that were consumed by the family at Chartwell. I heard the cook mention to a younger helper that during the war the plots also provided veggies for Number 10 Downing Street while Winston was prime minister.

I sometimes gnawed at tender greens. Usually I don't have much of an appetite for such except when my tummy is upset.

As I stood among roses in yellows, golds, and ochres, Grace came over and gestured at the thorny plants.

"The anniversary rose walk originated with Randolph's wish to honor his parents on their golden wedding anniversary. Both Winston and Clementine adored roses and had other extensive rose areas. However, since the flowers wouldn't be mature in time for the anniversary, Randolph commissioned a book containing paintings of yellow roses by celebrated artists," she informed.

I sniffed the fragrant air. These roses were real. I loved the aroma but knew better than to get too close to them. Fortunately, during my patrols in Winston's gardens, I didn't discover any encroachment of my territory by other cats.

I found an abundance of playthings worthy of energetic exertions. A large leaf pushed by the wind, a flower blossom that dried up and fell off its plant, the patch of lemon-scented catnip my human had planted—all allowed me to exercise my kitten instincts. I especially liked to nibble those gray-green oval leaves or doze among their aromatic branches.

I explored trees and shrubs near both the lower and upper lakes. Some of the more wooded areas were frequented by small rodents or birds. However, I felt less inclined to capture and eat wild game due to all the shared culinary delights I now had. In addition, the big man didn't like it when I hunted or caught birds. On occasion I did leave a trophy near the entrance to the old kitchen. Ordinarily an attendant removed this before I could carry it upstairs.

I also practiced my stalking and attacks. Winston was in his study sitting in the padded chair near the fireplace. I entered by the stairs and crouched down by his sit-down desk. I moved my head from side to side as I gauged my target. Then at the right moment, I sprang forward, lunging at my human. I took several rapid bounds then abruptly stopped in front of him. He laughed at my antics. He patted his lap, and I jumped up and licked his chin.

One place I avoided at all costs was the driveway in front of the house with the street beyond. That painful memory was deeply etched into my psyche. There would be excursions when I would travel with Winston back to his London home. On those rare occasions I would stand close to my slowly moving human in order to avoid dangers that could cause me harm.

Chapter 16

The Sinews of Peace

I heard several of Winston's attendants congratulating him on his decision not to stand for Parliament again. I think Clementine was more relieved than her husband. She always carried an exhausting burden of worrying about him.

One afternoon I followed Winston as he shuffled as quickly as he could across his study to his bedroom. Anthony Montague Browne, Winston's private secretary, had told him a storm was imminent. Like a young boy, my human was excited. I was not. I found a nice perch atop Winston's bed. He watched through the bay window as dark clouds swirled above the landscape and the lake he had created. Soon the tempest unleashed its fury, with lightning and thunder putting on a powerful display. The trees shook in the wind, and rain pelted the windows. When the storm subsided, he seemed to ebb as well.

Winston seems to be slowing down. When he sits down in his armchair, his shrunken body seems to hover before dropping heavily to the cushion. Similarly, when he rises to his feet, I can see him plant his feet firmly and then strain to push himself up with his scrawny arms. Roy's assistance is usually required now, especially when he walks.

Because of Winston's diminished condition, he has become more sluggish and easily fatigued.

"Jock, I wish I had your childlike energy," he sighed one afternoon. "Ah, to be twenty to twenty-five again, those were the years!"

Tears occasionally rolled down his cheeks. According to Anthony, he was never afraid to shed a tear in public. In more recent years his memory of his lost youth often made him weepy. I think he still wanted to make a difference in world affairs, but time and energy had forsaken him.

Most days he sits in silence and stares into the fire which burns even as the days are warming. I am less distressed by these developments than his family, friends, and attendants. When I met him, his decline had already begun. Others remembered the energy and zeal that he exuded until he left his second term as prime minister, but that was unknowable to me.

Despite the numerous inconveniences and frustrations associated with his reduced mobility, my human remained determined to get out and about. He lunched recently in the House of Commons dining room, site of many enjoyable meals.

"Like the First World War which stole so many of my friends and colleagues," Winston remembered to Clementine, "Thomas Moore's somber words have once again captured my sentiments. 'I feel like one who treads alone some banquet-hall deserted, whose lights are fled, whose garlands dead, and all but he departed.'"

In his mind's eye he could imagine the familiar faces, camaraderie, and repartee, but they were long absent. Winston had always been a man of bold, grand dreams. Now his memories ultimately surpassed his dreams in importance. That's discouraging for a person who once thrived on being the center of attention, commanding legions of faithful followers.

Foreign travel no longer promised him the adventure he previously enjoyed. Still, he departed to cruise from Monte Carlo on what Winston called his "monster yacht," a former Canadian naval frigate owned by a rich Greek benefactor. Randolph, young Winston his grandson, a granddaughter, and a number of close friends accompanied him. As before, Clementine did not go on what would be Winston's last cruise.

I missed my fur times and meals with him. Winston has a special way of rubbing me behind my ears. Then he runs both hands down my back from the base of my neck to the sides of my rear legs. After several long, slow rubs, I gently nibble on his fingers then brush my forehead across his face alternating each side.

Afterward, I press my front paws into his midsection exchanging paws until he chuckles. His lavender-scented hands are gentle now. We have both found ways to bring good cheer to the other.

"Jock, you're just what I need." he declared, giving me a thumb's-up gesture upon his return. He seemed physically drained from his travels. I, on the other hand, had an overabundance of energy and crouched down in an alert posture.

When I was a young kitten, I experienced the joys of simply being alive. My siblings and I would race around bumping into each other. We'd jump straight up into the air with exuberance. Each new discovery brought fresh delights. Butterflies and crawling insects demanded instant study. Falling leaves gathered in piles around our home became a source of merriment when we leaped into them. Even the wind that mysteriously moved tree branches was regarded with wonder and not fear.

Humans would still consider me a kitten with a zest for living. I am delighted at being able to run without growing weak. Possibly the big man was like that once, too.

Time has, however, not completely stolen his mental abilities. Although he speaks little, Roy says he's always thinking. Occasionally he remembers something from the past so exactly that I know he is reexperiencing that adventure.

A spry, bald, wizened man with a mustache visited Winston and stayed for several days. He spoke in a clipped, proper way. This visitor's upbeat presence, however, gave my human a lift. Afterward, I heard the Sergeant, who was discreetly watching the two men, remark that it was hard to believe that this ferret-like man, Field Marshal Bernard Law Montgomery, was Britain's best fighting general in the Second World War.

"Monty, take a snap of Jock, there."

The other man pointed his camera at me. I was more preoccupied with a lively orange butterfly with black spots and small blue dots sailing nearby.

"That's a small tortoiseshell, *Aglais urticae*, one of my favorite butterflies," Winston informed Monty. "Their preferred nectars are planted in the garden including buddleias, verbena bonariensis, and of course, lavender."

Unlike Winston's London home that had no lavender, I had discovered some here on my earlier travels, and those had become one of my favorite places to take a nap.

"Tortoiseshells favor violet and red flowers. I've been fascinated by butterflies since I was with the 4th Hussars in India before the turn of the century."

"Indeed, you were," was all Monty could utter, absolutely stunned by Winston's grasp of the details.

My human relished Monty's company. They liked to sit by the low stone wall that surrounded the terrace lawn. Wispy high clouds moved slowly across a pastel blue sky, and the trees rustled in a gentle breeze. The view of the many lakes and the scenic countryside at Chartwell complemented the companionship.

Winston sat in his basket chair, a comfortable cushion resting upon a wicker frame that sat atop two wheels. He wore his cowboy hat, a heavy coat, and a blanket to cover his body. I, of course, added to his warmth by sitting on his lap.

Suddenly a small black rabbit emerged from the bushes, its nose twitching as it smelled the air. I instantly got excited, because rabbits are much more challenging than butterflies. My ears became alert. I tensed my body ready to spring.

The creature was clearly too big to consider as food, but it might offer some excellent play opportunities.

I leaped toward it, but it was already in motion, sprinting away and changing direction abruptly several times without slowing down. I stopped my pursuit and then, to mask my lack of success, proceeded to lick myself. I wanted the others to think that I didn't really want to catch that rabbit.

Winston and Monty watched my spurt of activity without comment. I returned to my earlier resting spot and lay down.

Monty spoke rapidly, evidently distressed by the geopolitical challenges of the day. He kept mentioning something called NATO and emphasizing his belief that the nations that had won the big war were now losing the peace.

My human listened to him. Then, looking out across his emerald domain, he replied with a wry smile, "If the human race wishes to have a prolonged and indefinite period of material prosperity, they have only got to behave in a peaceful and helpful way toward one another, and science will do for them all that they wish and more than they can dream. Nothing is final."

He stammered as he thought about what came next. All the while, he gestured theatrically with his hands and arms as if he were orating to a group. "Ah," he sighed.

Finding his place, he continued, "Change is unceasing, and it is likely that mankind has a lot more to learn before it comes to its journey's end. We might even find ourselves in a few years moving along a smooth causeway of peace and plenty instead of roaming around on the rim of hell. Thus, we may by patience, courage, and in orderly progression reach the shelter of a calmer and kindlier age."

Monty's mouth fell open. "Bravo, Winston!" he exclaimed.

"That was from my 'Sinews of Peace' speech." Winston paused with a smile and his eyes twinkling. Then he concluded with, "The future is unknowable, but the past should give us hope."

I spent my time grooming myself because I understood little of what was said. Winston's voice, however, was strong, rich, and full of expression. I had never heard an oration of such power and majesty. It was as if, for an instant, time had returned the former gifts that he had so powerfully possessed.

Chapter 17

The Unknown War

FIRST she cleared her throat, knowing that her father didn't like to be surprised by a sudden voice. A pause then Mary said, "You're looking well this morning, Papa." Mary exaggerated, as she always did, by saying "Pa-pah."

I was curled up on Winston's lap. I watched as his daughter sat beside him on the couch in the drawing room.

She patted my back and said, "And how are you today, Mr. Moggy?"

I made a little chirp as she touched me then returned my head to my crossed paws.

The big man nodded as he studied his daughter. Removing his cigar from his lips, he replied, "My life is so sedate these days. I am reduced to idleness and memories."

"Papa, you've earned your right to take it easier now. You've lived such an adventurous life." She was serious by nature, but today she wanted to keep things light and upbeat.

"In my mind's eye I see my youthful exploits. The Malakand Field Force, the cavalry charge at Omdurman, the armored train and my escape from the Boers, riding with the South African Light Horse, Spion Kop, even the trenches on the Western Front at Plugstreet."

Suddenly he stopped, and with a twinkle in his eye, lapsed into song.

"Wrap me up in me old tarpaulin jacket
And say a poor buffer lies low.
Get six stalwart Lancers to carry me,
With steps mournful, solemn, and slow."

"Papa," Mary laughed, "when did you sing that?"

"With my battalion of the 6th Royal Scots Fusiliers in the trenches in 1916. Those were exciting times!

"When it comes to fighting, what I observed years ago is still true, nothing in life is so exhilarating as to be shot at without result."

Mary listened thoughtfully as did I, my head up with my eyes slowly blinking—cat kisses—to my human whom I adore.

"Those were lively deeds before I assumed greater responsibilities for the safety of the nation. My wartime travels were quite the adventure, too.

By battleship, flying boat, and bomber, we skirted the periphery of the Nazi dominion to meet the other Allied leaders."

"Which trip was most challenging?"

"Flying tens of thousands of miles in a cold, unheated, uncomfortable bomber bay was trying for a man of my age. But it needed to be done. That was my duty and my destiny."

As Winston spoke, I saw the color of his face take on a deeper hue. He was more engaged and looked more alive. I think Mary observed this, too, and she continued to draw him out.

"Were you ever frightened?" she asked.

"Frightened, never!" He repeated it for emphasis, "Never! Apprehensive? Often! Whenever I flew, there always was a chance of being shot down or the plane having an equipment malfunction. Similarly, there was a possibility of getting torpedoed in submarine-infested waters. My perils, however, paled compared to what our men faced on the front lines, fighting and dying in bitter struggles against an unwavering enemy."

"Ever have any big regrets during the war?" Mary inquired.

"I had wanted to observe the D-Day landing from the cruiser, *Belfast*. I liked to be where the action was regardless of the risk. General Eisenhower, Ike as I called him, was dead set against it and persuaded the King to prevent me. Ultimately, I had to obey my Sovereign."

"I remember coming back with you from the Quebec Conference on *HMS Renown*," Mary recalled. "They celebrated my twenty-first birthday with a cake and later drinks in the wardroom. I felt so grown up."

"That was 1943, the fourth year of the war," Winston added.

"Afterward I was on deck in the late afternoon," Mary continued. "The area where we stood was actually off limits for safety reasons. The air was bracing, and the seas were bounding. During one of our zigzags, I lost my footing as the ship rolled. A wall of green water struck me and swept me across the deck toward the outboard edge. I realized that if I went overboard in those seas, I would be lost. By the time I grasped the seriousness of my impending doom, I was thankfully stopped by the lifeline and nearby stanchion.

"You should have seen the look of concern and gravity in the faces of my shipboard friends! I was taken below and given a stiff brandy followed by a scotch."

"A most appropriate remedy," Winston inserted.

"Since I only had but one uniform and it was drenched by sea water, I wore civilian clothes to supper in the wardroom that night. I incurred your reprimand since I was your *aide-de-camp* and out of uniform.

"And, Papa," she paused, "I'm sorry. I should have told you sooner of my ordeal."

"Mouse," his voice trailed off.

"You haven't called me that in years, Papa."

I looked around hoping to see a fuzzy, quick-moving creature scurrying nearby. Seeing nothing, I scratched the side of my face with my left rear paw.

"Mouse, that's water over the dam, or should I say, over the deck, now," he replied with surprising quickness. "I'm glad you were safely rescued.

"Remember," his tone growing more serious, "war is a game to be played with a smiling face even when there is no laughter in your heart."

Looking at Mary, I sensed she thought his words were harsh, but she realized in a time of crisis, a leader had to be firm and pragmatic.

She was mute for a moment then replied, "I do understand, Papa. A stiff upper lip instills hope in the hearts of one's followers."

"Just so," Winston responded with a smile.

Chapter 18

The Unwritten Alliance

I was catnapping next to the night nurse on duty in Winston's study when I heard noises coming from downstairs. My ears swiveled in the direction of the sounds. Cats can discern higher pitched sounds beyond what humans and even dogs can detect. We can hear the minute squeaks mice make as they rustle through the underbrush. We can also pinpoint in three dimensions the source of sounds so accurately that our hunting abilities are optimized.

I jumped off the armchair and quickly padded downstairs. Near the entrance hall were Grace and Clementine. In spite of the late hour, Grace seemed to be dressed for working in the garden, even with her wellies, while Clementine wore bedclothes with a pink robe belted around her waist. The front double doors were open, and a strongly-built man was lugging a large framed painting outside into the cool, late evening air.

Grace reached over and patted Clementine's arm, saying, "We have this under control. My brother will ensure that this hideous likeness of your husband disappears forever."

"Are you sure?" Clementine asked. "Parliament was so keen about Sutherland's portrait as a gift on Winston's eightieth birthday. His canvas was, however, unkind, a gross mockery of him! Although Winston joked that it was a fine example of modern art, he loathed it. It's been hidden all these years in the basement."

"Don't worry. We'll take care of this."

I followed the procession and watched as the man with huge hands hefted the painting into the back of a van.

Grace noticed my presence, and as if reading my mind said, "Jock, want to come along?" She patted the bed of the van next to where the framed canvas lay.

I jumped up and rested on a nearby folded blanket. Grace's brother closed the rear doors to the van. He and Grace then got in and closed their doors. The engine started, and the van sped through the night.

"It's late, Gracie. No one will see us. A few more miles and we'll have this artistic trash stewing in its own juices."

"No one will suspect anything," Grace agreed. "Your house is a much better place for this mischief than Chartwell."

"Right as pie. We'll do the deed in my secluded garden. I've already dug a deep hole and placed ample wood around it."

Grace's brother parked the van and swung open the doors. He then carried the painting around the side of the house and into the yard. It was pitch black out, but I could see much better than the two humans could. I walked alongside Grace, who pulled her sweater tight around her body.

Her brother placed the painting in the center of the pit and stoked some logs against it. He then doused it and the logs with petrol. The volatile vapors made my nose twitch, and I sneezed twice.

"Stand back, Gracie. Grab the cat, too."

Grace picked me up and took several steps away. Her brother lit a match and threw it into the pit. With a noisy rush, flames leaped into the sky. Heat radiated outward. Despite the warmth of the fire, Grace kept her sweater wrapped around her, shivering more from her indiscretion than from the air temperature. The bonfire burned with tremendous intensity, greedily consuming its midnight snack.

"I wish Clementine could see this!" she told her brother. "I'll tell her about it tomorrow, but I'll not say anything to Winston. He must be protected from our actions."

I watched the flames devour the oil painting and its ornate frame. Flickering orange light danced across the faces of Grace and her brother. The three of us were partners in justice.

Chapter 19

Stemming the Tide

"IS he...?" Clementine asked, her voice breaking into a sob which she quickly stifled.

"Dying?" the doctor said. "If that's what you're asking, I'll not sugar-coat it."

"Charles, you never do," she snapped, her voice rising in pitch like it did when she got emotional. Then regretted her sharp tone. Grace had informed me that Charles Wilson, also known as Lord Moran, had been Winston's physician ever since he was prime minister during the war.

"Yes, Winston's condition is critical."

I eavesdropped on the conversation they were having in the study, sufficiently removed from my human's bedroom.

"Winston's suffered another mild stroke. Not as severe as the one he had a decade earlier during his second premiership. He may bounce back, but he's much older now."

"What can we do to help him recover?" she inquired.

"I suggest he regain his strength by remaining confined to bed."

"He won't make it easy. You know how stubborn he can be."

Throughout the morning Winston remained unmoving, reading neither book nor newspaper, and not uttering a decipherable word. This condition continued for several days.

I became more assertive and jumped onto Winston's bed, despite Roy's preference that I give my human some space. He was propped up by several pillows. His body seemed smaller than before. A thin smile told me he recognized me. I lay down beside him, purring to comfort him.

Later that day I noticed Clementine about to walk into Winston's bedroom. She took a deep breath before she entered as if she were preparing herself to be positive with him about his declining health. I took my normal short breath and followed her in.

Monty came by to cheer him up. He showed him some photos taken of them during both wars. Winston's eyes lit up when he saw the pictures. He was wearing one of his one-piece siren suits. He always wore his special blue and white polka dot bow tie just as I always wore my blue collar. We were two peas in a pod!

"Do you recognize this snap, Winston?" Monty asked.

Winston started at the photo then haltingly exclaimed, "That was taken during the previous war when London troops paraded into Lille a couple weeks before the 1918 Armistice. Oh, there's Eddie Marsh, my private secretary, behind me." He didn't mention anyone else.

"And there I am," said Monty proudly, "a dapper lieutenant-colonel standing just in front of you. That's probably the first picture taken of us together."

Winston didn't comment on their joint appearance. But he remembered, "Later that same afternoon as we headed up to tour the front, I saw a village church with a most alluring steeple. I coaxed General," he paused, "ah, Tudor, yes, General Tudor, to climb to the top and survey the German lines. It wasn't long before their heavy artillery rounds whizzed over our heads. Then we caught a whiff of mustard gas. We beat a quick strategic withdrawal."

Monty was again astonished by his friend's amazing recall even after suffering a stroke.

The intermittent rain from the past few days stopped, and the sun reappeared. A faint rainbow hung in the sky, ending over Winston's studio, a good omen.

The daylight coming through the bay window, the good conversation, and the wartime snapshots worked their magic. My human smiled and seemed more animated. He never had any problem hearing Monty's crisp, commanding voice.

A housemaid brought tea for Monty since the big man still had a glass partially filled with whisky so diluted with soda that it looked like water. There were scones, Dundee Cake, and clotted cream. I'm partial to the clotted cream, but Winston immediately reached for the Dundee Cake. The food revived both men.

Later Monty mentioned to Anthony, "He's definitely on the mend. He will recover!" Under his breath, the general muttered, "I'm more worried about Clementine. She's worn out and needs rest."

Winston continued to improve as the days went by. I was beside him on the bed more than usual. I sat down on the pile of his unread newspapers. When he attempted to move me, I nibbled at his fingers. I wouldn't give an inch. He chuckled at my playfulness. I was happy to get such a positive reaction from him.

Soon he was getting up and stiffly yet slowly walking around in his study. I accompanied him, and from time to time he stopped and smiled down at me. We both liked the airy feeling that the vaulted ceiling with the exposed beams and rafters brought to that refuge. Here he had created most of his important literary works, rehearsed speeches, and devised strategies for countering foreign enemies.

Chapter 20

Thoughts and Adventures

THE next night after dinner, Winston watched a movie in his basement cinema. I sat on the settee near Clementine but not too close. She only tapped me briefly on my head, not a dismissal but not a caress either. I climbed atop a pile of large film cans and perched there after the entertainment ended.

One morning as I lay curled at my human's feet, a housemaid delivered a letter to him. He was well enough to read it aloud: "My darling Winston, today we have been married 55 years." He placed it on the bed, and I noticed there was a small picture of a cat drawn at the bottom of her letter. It was clearly from Clementine, and it cheered him immensely.

His wife had been his homeport whether his life held clear blue skies or darkened storms. She was the center of Winston's emotional existence. She cared about him, his health, and his reputation.

Anthony, Winston's troubleshooter, invited a number of the big man's friends over, but individually so as to not wear him out. Among them was my savior and namesake, Mr. Jock. I greeted him warmly, rubbing my sides against his legs. He reached down and tickled me behind the ears.

"You seem to be thriving, Mr. Cat. I'm more than convinced I made the right decision in rescuing you. I know Winston is quite attached to you."

After watching a movie one night with me his only companion, Winston wrote to his grandson, asking him to visit. By Churchillian tradition, fathers and sons alternated naming their children with each successive generation. Accordingly, both Winston's father and son were named Randolph. Winston's grandson was also Winston S. Churchill. He was called Winston by those close to him and young Winston by the staff—interesting that no one called my human "old Winston."

Young Winston came by the next week. In his early twenties, he was following in his grandfather's journalistic footsteps. Together they discussed in detail some of the photos of his African odyssey he had previously sent to his grandfather.

Young Winston was always kind to me. I'm not sure he had an affinity for felines, but he did love his grandfather to whom I belonged. He usually rubbed me under my collar, a place I can't easily reach. I think Winston enjoyed his presence more than that of his own son, Randolph, because his grandson never argued with him. In addition both Winston and young Winston had notable exploits in their early lives.

Soon we were ready for our annual pilgrimage back to Winston's London home for the colder months. It was quite an ordeal. Grace coordinated with housemaids, nurses, butlers, and drivers to launch a caravan of four cars and countless pieces of luggage. I rode in the seat next to him in his black Humber Pullman. He, as usual, was impatient with the driver going too slowly. He'd call out, "Go on! Now! Be quick about it, go!" It was sunny and dry, but the days were noticeably shorter and the daylight weaker.

At the townhouse I walked through the entrance and into the drawing room, reacquainting myself with the old smells. Winston entered and sat down heavily in his armchair next to the fire. "Jock, that trip has become arduous," he shared. "Let me catch my breath."

He commanded the butler to throw on some additional logs. He then prodded them with his walking stick until the fire blazed warmly.

Clementine was in the hospital being treated for exhaustion when their daughter Mary stopped by. She hesitated uncomfortably then told him that Diana had taken her own life. Winston just sat there letting the devastating news sink in. He was too overwhelmed with sadness to speak.

Mary saw me looking at my human and quietly revealed to me that for the second occasion in his life, he had outlived a daughter. He spoke not a word nor shed a tear, but I could sense he experienced great despair. It was written all over his ashen face. The nursing and housekeeping staff tiptoed around, afraid to encroach on his sorrow.

The tears came later as he sat there alone with a faraway look, bewildered by the unhappy events. Winston muttered to himself his daughter's nickname, "Poor Puppy Kitten."

I offered him the only consolation I could, my presence. I leaned against his leg and rubbed my head against him. I made shallow meowing sounds. Winston withdrew deeply inside himself. His golden years were being tarnished by the heavy burdens he bore.

Days passed. Clementine, now home, raced into her husband's bedroom, disturbing his afternoon nap with the news that President Kennedy had been shot in Dallas. As I lay alongside his legs, he seemed stunned. Was he thinking back to mid-year when he, with me on his lap, watched on television as the youthful president made him an honorary American citizen? After dinner, he just gazed into the fire as he reflected on Kennedy's shocking end.

Winston's eighty-ninth birthday was followed by successive holidays—Christmas, Boxing Day, and New Year's Day—which occurred without much fanfare. I'm not much for holidays, but I do enjoy the extra food treats that humans feel compelled to share with me.

One day as Winston was sitting in the drawing room, he said, "Jock, you don't look down on me, do you?"

I looked at him quizzically and bent around to lick myself.

He continued, "I once stated, dogs look up to you, cats look down on you, but give me a pig! A pig looks you in the eye and treats you as an equal. I think you treat me as an equal and sometimes you look me in the eye, too."

I lifted up my rear leg and continued to clean myself.

Winston sat wordlessly for a while then spoke to me again. "You're my best listener, Jock. And you never disagree with me."

A half smile crossed his face. "I wish I had your fur; I'd be warmer."

I considered that an invitation and made myself comfortable on his lap.

The weather turned markedly colder with some drizzle and even a little snow. I have grown to dislike snow. I freely admit I'm a fair-weather feline.

One of the housemaids put into vases vibrantly hued flowers that were regularly delivered from Winston's country home. Despite being a lackluster day, the blossoms gave off both color and fragrance that brightened the surroundings by recreating for Winston a little bit of his beloved Chartwell.

Whenever it was sunny and mild, however, I took to the garden on the other side of our tall fence. I needed to reconnect with the neighborhood friends I hadn't seen in some time. And I wanted to keep the small terrier honest by teasing him. Whenever I got him barking at night, the lights came on in the back of his house. What fun!

Chapter 21

Closing the Ring

EVEN the English winter with its snows, sleet, and rain couldn't keep big man homebound. I've heard others say he showed great resilience throughout his long life, being flexible and alert for opportunities for self-renewal. He sounds very much like a cat to me. These activities allowed him, and me, to bounce back from adversity, which he needed more than ever now.

One day he paused while enjoying the outside view and said to me, "Jock, I have done my bit. I should be allowed to depart in peace."

Where did he want to visit? He was impatient and still wanted to determine his destiny. Cats want to drive their own trains, too. Nonetheless, I took the occasion to lick Winston's fingers which he seemed to appreciate.

Roy and the housemaids had to prepare Winston for multiple travels to the House of Commons as well as to excursions to the Other Club, a political dining club founded by Winston and a friend almost half a century earlier. During his visits away from his home, he rarely walked. If the venue required any effort beyond what dwindling reserves he possessed, he was pushed in a wheelchair. He invariably leaned on a colleague's arm while using his walking stick. He was not only slowing down more but finding it increasingly difficult to move around at all.

Once he went to the theatre in South London to see his daughter Sarah perform. I was nearby when Grace and Anthony discussed the experience afterward. Sarah had played the lead role in the theatrical production.

The festive occasion was awkwardly marred as Winston and Clementine were placed in the front row, and the high stage obscured their view of their daughter. Winston craned his head to see but eventually settled back and took in the show from its ankle-high perspective.

Nonetheless, after the show, a buoyant Winston was wheeled backstage to greet Sarah and her friends. He winked and smiled at several of the pretty faces among the cast. He was given a cigar as well as a whisky and soda. Afterward the cast toasted his health with champagne.

I sensed from Grace's words that Sarah liked playing the parts of different people. In fact, humans in general seem to find satisfaction in assuming another's character. As a cat, I cannot imagine being anyone but myself. I wonder if Winston ever assumed different roles.

This was a much happier occurrence than one I observed previously. Sarah had returned to Chartwell after burying her third husband, Henry, in Spain where they had lived. Winston met her at the front door. When she arrived just before lunch, her grief was still raw, and tears filled her eyes when she saw him. I stood silently at his feet watching.

Winston and his daughter said nothing at first, simply looking at each other. Then I saw him reach out and take Sarah's hands, almost a duplicate of his delicate ones.

"We must close ranks and move on," he said. Then he added, "My poor Mule."

Sarah eventually nodded as tears spilled down her pale cheeks. Hearing her childhood nickname further touched her heart.

The recently resigned prime minister, Harold Macmillan, came to visit and partake of a roast beef lunch. He had a dangling mustache and wavy grey hair over his ears. The cook made an especially delicious Yorkshire pudding, light and fluffy. After lunch, they both departed for the

House of Commons to hear the new prime minister at Question Time.

On many of these occasions Winston was wonderfully present and chatty, having clear recollections of events that had occurred in his youth. These times regrettably became less frequent.

The details the big man remembered meant nothing to me. Often his words were recognizable but on occasion they might become slurred as if his tongue were too thick. His ability to follow a conversation varied, too, as his hearing worsened. The activity of talking and listening wore him out. Still, he relished visits from old friends.

My savior, Mr. Jock, and his wife visited again for supper. I was eager to present myself knowing I'd get some appropriate recognition, what they referred to in the military as being "mentioned in dispatches." I was not disappointed.

When Randolph came to dinner, I ducked around the corner and hid under the bed. Providentially, nothing untoward occurred on this occasion.

Winston, Clementine, and the entire entourage traveled to Chartwell early this year for Easter. The morning we arrived was cold with fog that cast an opaque veil across the picturesque landscape. Not long afterward, we had some snow that removed my familiar smells. I'd have to start from scratch when things dried up.

In some ways Winston, too, started over each time he returned to his country home. And he was progressively more in need of the rejuvenating effect it had on him.

Chapter 22

Keep Right on to the End

AS I matured as a cat, I realized that the number of imponderables grew rather than diminished. For example, why do humans send for the dog catcher to capture stray cats? Why do they call it teatime when Winston only drinks coffee? How come there are no cat days of summer? Similarly, why are the pointed, killing, and shredding teeth in my mouth called canines? Unless I overheard others discussing these, I remained clueless.

Randolph once claimed that cats weren't much smarter than ducks. If that's so, why do millions of people spoil cats as pets yet eat ducks?

Another puzzle intrigued me. The big man generously shared his sumptuous repasts with me. I grew fond of beef Wellington, Nelson's mutton cutlets, Salisbury steak, eggs Benedict, oysters Rockefeller, Napoleons, Caesar salad, and Kaiser rolls. I wondered if there were any foods named after Winston. Even Clementine had a fruit named after her.

Once I sat in the kitchen where the cook explained to an assistant my human's eating preferences.

"Sir Winston likes his beef steaks cooked medium and his roast beef rare."

Frankly, I am not particular about how my meat is cooked. I'll take it any way at all including raw, although Winston is not a tartare fan.

He's very picky about what he likes and dislikes. He enjoys Dundee cake but not currant cake. He prefers canned mandarin oranges but not marmalade. He relishes apple fritters but not apple tarts. Indian curries were in, but Chinese food was out, and chocolate mousse was okay, but chocolates were not. We both agreed that black pudding should never darken our breakfast plate.

People have realized that cats aren't vanilla creatures like dogs. We have more discerning tastes and choose whom we befriend. We don't typically do tricks like fetching balls or sticks, rolling over, or shaking with our paws.

I am who I am, and that's all that I am. I'm never bad—well, not too often. I'm just being a cat. I love Winston unconditionally, so I have modified some of my independent ways. My human, may he always be right, but when wrong, he's still my human.

Winston once told Anthony, "Man is spirit." The two men were sitting in Winston's library, a room about half the size of the drawing room. The floor-to-ceiling bookcase was overflowing with books. The lingering smell of cigar smoke permeated the space.

Anthony replied that since Noah on the ark saved cats as well, no doubt they had a soul, too. While people might be unsure, I was not.

Winston sat in an orangish upholstered chair sandwiched between his wooden writing desk and the bookcase wall. He played with his unlit cigar. Anthony lounged in a wooden arm chair next to him. Since the other padded chair on the opposite side of the mahogany writing table was unoccupied, I curled up on it. The nearby fireplace warmed the room and kept me very comfortable.

Cats have a sixth sense when it comes to life. We can feel an aura that each creature exudes. We simply acknowledge its presence the same way we take for granted the air we breathe.

In a similar vein, people like to think we cats have nine lives. We realize that's a clever way of saying we're lucky. As I have said before, felines land on their feet both physically and metaphorically. The only life I know is the one I'm living.

I turned and studied Winston's desk. He had photos and other interesting knick- knacks on it. I'd been up on it before, but now I decided to clean my paws and spread all my little toes out widely to facilitate my primping.

That night I was lying next to Winston in his bed. Instead of slumbering off, he must have been considering the discussion he had had with Anthony earlier in the day.

He looked in my direction and said, "I've only prayed twice in my life, Jock." His hand reached over and stroked the back of my head as I purred.

He added, "Once was the day after I escaped from the State Model School where I was a prisoner of the Boers, finding myself three hundred miles inside enemy territory. And the other, the day I saw your limp and bleeding body after you were struck by that car."

He continued rubbing me a little longer. "And both of my prayers were wonderfully answered." His hand slowed and a snore soon seeped from his lips.

The next day as I returned from patrolling my gardens, I found Winston with Anthony again.

The younger man was a loyal assistant. He played cards with his boss, handled his correspondence, and kept him company. In addition, he also handled many of Winston's financial matters.

Like me, he saw Winston at his best and worst. But the best was truly scintillating! At his worst, it was sad because my human's ears and lower limbs refused their office.

In a flash of lucidity, the big man intoned, "So I drew these tides of men into my hands and wrote my will across the sky in stars."

"Sir Winston, where did you say that?" Anthony asked. I think he knew perfectly well but always looked for ways to give him some small victory.

"I didn't, but I think it applies equally well to me. My friend T.E. Lawrence, the famous Lawrence of Arabia, composed that for the dedication of his extraordinary book, *The Seven Pillars of Wisdom*."

Winston began to cough. After a short bout, he recovered his breath and continued, "You know, he was my Middle East advisor in 1921 when I was at the Colonial Office. We rode camels together in front of the pyramids."

I assumed a sphinx-like pose with my eyes half shut. The wind gently rustled the trees, and I caught a scent of flowers dancing lightly on the air.

"Later, during my wilderness years, Lawrence used to arrive here on his motorcycle on Sunday afternoons for tea and often stayed for dinner. Once to Mary's enchantment, he came downstairs in the robes of a prince of Arabia."

Anthony smiled, knowing Winston was happy from having such a vivid memory. I was delighted since my Winston was back.

Chapter 23

Great Contemporaries

We journeyed back to London after only two months at Chartwell. Anthony told me Winston was unable to attend the opening of Churchill College, Cambridge, which he founded years before, but Clementine represented him at the event.

I was sitting on Winston's bed when I heard a knock on the door. Anthony entered and strode over to his boss, who was reading a newspaper.

"Sir Winston, I regret to tell you that Max is dead. We have just heard. I'm sorry."

I looked over and saw the newspaper fall to the bed as my human bowed his head without saying a word. He seemed in shock.

According to Anthony, Max Aitken, the Lord Beaverbrook, had been one of Winston's closest friends for almost six decades. As Prime Minister in 1940, Winston had appointed Beaverbrook as Minister of Aircraft Production because of his singular ability to get things done.

He put badly needed planes in the sky for "the Few," Winston's heroic Royal Air Force pilots. By their courage, they maintained air superiority over the Nazis and thereby prevented England from being invaded. Winston had then quipped, "Some people take drugs; I take Max!"

My human grieved in silence, as was his way.

Days passed. No doubt he was reliving pleasant moments he had shared with Max. Once, however, he chuckled at a memory. He recounted to Mary a race up the long stairway at Beaverbrook's villa in the south of France.

Both men were in their eighties. Winston rode up the electric chair-lift, and Max on foot climbed the stairs. Every few steps Winston stopped the lift to allow his oldest of friends to catch up. Both gentlemen had been competitive when they were younger, but now their congeniality and companionship meant more to them than winning.

I certainly approved Winston's generosity overcoming his desire to claim the limelight.

The loss of those dear to him created a sad atmosphere of depression over the townhome. Anthony mentioned that the "Big Three" friends in Winston's life were gone—Lord Cherwell, also known as "the Prof," Brendan Bracken, and now Max.

The Prof had helped Winston understand terribly complex scientific and technical concepts. Brendan, who had assisted in both political and financial matters, liked to tease Winston, to Clementine's annoyance, by claiming that he was his illegitimate son.

The housemaids and nurses were respectful, maintaining a low profile to avoid intruding on his personal grief. As I always did, I moved like a shadow. I never acted flashy or attracted attention. It was simply not my way. Instead, I kept him company throughout these difficult periods. I lay next to him and leaned up against him. I wanted him to feel my presence.

Winston soon caught a cold that persisted for more than a week. His energy level was already low, and this recent affliction sapped his strength even further.

Eventually he was on the mend. It was a sunny and mild afternoon, so we sat in the garden. He read a book about sculpture while I chased the butterflies that hovered over some bright purple flowers.

He looked up, and there standing next to him was his grandson. His deafness had prevented him from hearing the back door open and close.

"Congratulations and happiness," Winston said, a smile spreading across his upturned face as he remembered young Winston's recent engagement. Then he looked back down at his book. A minute or so went by as he read, then he looked up again. His grandson was still standing there, a little uncomfortable.

"Come with me to my room," he commanded, and Roy wheeled him inside. After he got into bed, he asked for his checkbook on the dresser. He found he had no pen. I hopped up next to him while the grandson stood nearby.

"Let me borrow your pen," he said to the young man. Then after a series of gyrations involving a secretary, written checks, consultations with his wife via a female secretary, a number of "Nos" from the big man, and a signature, a check was finally handed to his grandson.

The young man looked at the amount and was overwhelmed by the generosity.

"Grandpapa, I'm speechless! I can't thank you enough. I can't wait for you to meet my bride-to-be, a sweet girl. I look forward to bringing her to luncheon with you next Sunday."

"My boy," he said, "I hope you'll both live, like Clemmie and me, happily ever after. And as I have learned over a long life, never flinch, never weary, never despair."

"I'll never forget, grandpapa," he promised.

Winston was pleased with his grandson's delight at the substantial gift, a token of his approval of the upcoming marriage. I purred contently alongside him in concurrence.

After the wedding, which Winston and Clementine were unable to attend, the entire clan of the two united families arrived at Winston's London home for a special reception. Pol Roger champagne flowed as the happy couple, parents, and grandparents celebrated the nuptial.

I overheard a nurse describe the subsequent fiasco. Chairs were set up in the garden for a group photograph. Winston sat front and center, flanked by his grandson on his left and granddaughter-in-law on his right. Clementine stood looking over her husband's left shoulder. More than a dozen others were arranged nearby. A rather famous and distinguished photographer from Canada had his camera ready to snap the photos when the big man asked, "Where's Jock?"

Inopportunely, because of all the commotion and also because Randolph was present, I had decided to go absent without leave. I was over the fence spending some time with my cat friends.

Housemaids, nurses, the bodyguard, and cooks looked everywhere in the two townhomes. They even checked the bedroom closet beneath my human's clothes. That was a backup hiding place I frequently used.

Things got tense. The young newlyweds had a larger function to attend after this more intimate reception. And I was putting a crimp in the flow of events.

From behind the wall I could hear the frantic cries and calls. Winston spoke loudly, "We won't take any snaps until Jock returns!" My ears jumped to attention when I heard my name.

At his summons, I quickly shimmied up the tree outside the wall, came over the stone wall, and clambered down the tree on the other side into the garden. Usually I come down bottom-first by straddling the trunk with my arms and hopping with my legs. But since I wanted to appear more dignified, I descended headfirst and landed completely balanced on all four paws. Perfect!

All eyes were on me. With my tail standing tall, I slowly walked over to my human, who patted his lap. I jumped up and then sat comfortably atop his legs.

Gathering me with his left hand and placing his right, still clutching his cigar, over my back, he said to the photographer in a weak voice, "Yousuf, you may continue." I turned my head so my best profile faced the camera.

A while later, Winston went to Parliament in the Palace of Westminster for the last time. As they departed for the House of Commons, Anthony congratulated him for his sixty-plus years as a member. I led the parade out the front door as the flashbulbs popped and the crowd cheered. He, with his cigar in his left hand and and steadying himself with his walking stick in the right, acknowledged the excitement of the press and other onlookers.

The next day as he read the newspaper, Winston pointed to a photograph of himself on the front page. "Look here," he said. "There's Jock."

And so I was, proudly walking ahead of him.

Chapter 24

In the Balance

OUR second return to Winston's country house this year was now a familiar ritual. Like a beneficent tornado, a frenzy of activity occurred prior to the move. Finally, all the bags were loaded, the humans embarked, and in a rush the caravan headed southeast to Kent. After we arrived and the motor cars had been unloaded, a quiet surrounded the household. The entire demeanor of living relaxed once we reentered the country refuge.

Like Winston, I regarded Chartwell as a sanctuary from an unpredictable world. The pace of life slowed down. Surprisingly, I never experienced a boring day at Winston's country home, and I think my human felt the same way.

In better times Winston presided over his domain like a feudal lord. He had used his own hands to construct extensive brick walls and the power of his imagination to direct the dredging of his swimming pool, lakes, and ponds. Each season here brought a feast of delight to his senses as he surveyed his work in every direction.

Creatures of all kinds occupied the paradise he created. Their unrehearsed antics and unselfconscious natures appealed to him. He had Siberian geese and Australian black swans—to me simply big birds—who ate the pieces of stale bread he threw to them. Foxes ate several of these graceful creatures—better them than me! This was a reminder that danger was always present, even in this idyllic setting.

Most humans do not realize that cats have the ability to traverse great distances. Psi trailing, magnetic fields, and the angle of the sun are involved in this process. Luckily, I'm rarely out of sight of Chartwell's chimneys so I didn't need to rely on these.

As spring transformed into summer, the greens deepened from pastel hues into pulsating lush ones—jades, teals, emeralds, chartreuses, aquamarines, shamrocks, and viridians. At least that's how my human with his eye for color described them. To me they were simply greens—light, medium, and dark.

We sat in the afternoon sunlight. Winston sighed, and his chin sank to his chest. From his lap, I looked up at him. His azure eyes, once so full of animation and inquisitiveness, were now subdued.

The palette of his life, formerly composed of vibrant, bold colors, had retreated to a monotone of muted grays.

"Jock, I'm tired," he whispered. "I wasn't always this way. There was a time ..." His voice trailed off, then he added, "What is there to live for when my last book has been written and my last painting has been completed? Imagine not having anything clever to say either."

I rubbed my forehead again his head. He looked directly at me. "Thank you, Jock." I purred with pleasure.

Next to me, I think the big man regarded his golden orfe as his second love. He fed his oversized goldfish maggots from a blue baby-food can, one lid for the juvenile orfe and several for the adults.

Roy, ever devoted even to such mundane tasks, assisted in ensuring the maggots were available and ready for use. These arrived at the local train station twice a month and were conveyed to Chartwell.

I watched the colorful spectacle unfold as Winston called out to his fish, "Arf! Arf!"

I'm convinced the fish recognized their benefactor and competed for his attention as he sat next to the pond. When they were sufficiently responsive and respectful, he'd throw them some breadcrumbs, too. He never tired of the sight of his orfe displaying their flashes of color.

He could no longer navigate on his unsteady limbs the undulating terrain near his fish ponds. Therefore, he did his traveling in a wheelchair propelled either by Roy, the Sergeant, or possibly even a visitor. I let the people go first and dutifully brought up the rear. Actually, that was the safer tactic. I never wanted to get chased down by Winston's runaway chair.

Monty joined us on one occasion. We passed through the front door and walked all the way down the long face of the house to the iron gate at the other side. Winston's wheelchair, however, was too wide to squeeze through the opening. Roy suggested that he fold it temporarily. He would assist Winston walking through the gate.

Winston, however, still a dogged and single-minded individual, insisted on sitting in his chair. He thought he could cross the open threshold if Roy and Monty tipped his chariot. He huffed, they puffed, and thankfully he and his chair managed to maneuver through the opening. To celebrate the I-told-you-so moment Winston shouted, "There you are, you see!" Clementine would have called him stubborn.

Monty was not surprised. Being stubborn was certainly a virtue when Winston refused to cower before Hitler. So was Winston's undeniable courage. Just thinking about this makes me proud to be an English cat!

Winston sat quietly as he fed his fish. I peered at the fish from the grassy threshold of the pond, my tail swishing from one side to the other. I could probably catch and eat one of those baby ones. I could tell my human was trying to recollect something.

"Do you see Jock there at the water's edge?" he asked.

"I do, Winston."

"You and I have both been standing together near the water on other more significant periods in history. Remind you of anything?"

Monty was still then laughed. "Ah, yes, that spring day in 1945 before the picnic lunch with Brookie—your esteemed Field Marshal Alan Brooke—and me. You walked over to the bank of the Rhine and relieved yourself. Rather a dramatic way to show your disdain for Hitler and his Nazis, I should think!"

A devilish smile crossed Winston's weary face. "Another finest hour!" he chirped. Then he raised his chin with the protruding cigar to Roy and said, "Howes, give me a light."

Chapter 25

Painting as a Pastime

MANY people consider Winston a national hero. Because of this, they often ascribe to him supernatural powers. I, however, see him in different terms. He is but a man yet a kind, decent, and generous one.

Like everyone, he has feet of clay. He can be inconsiderate, snappish, and gruff, particularly with those who feed, dress, and serve him. He's easily frustrated because his legs and hearing have let him down. Despite all his shortcomings, he is loved and respected.

Clementine once said to me, "Of course we indulge him. We always have, and we always will!"

When he's sleeping, I regularly join him. He is becoming more cat-like in his frequent napping. Today after he was snoozing, however, I wanted to inspect the grounds. I'm simply curious to see if any other creatures have invaded my domain.

I found the studio door open on this occasion. Grace was inside talking to a young journalist who was writing an article about Winston's favorite hobby, oil painting.

The walls were covered with hundreds of his paintings. Bright sunlight spilled through the many windows causing a rainbow of dazzling colors to reflect from the canvases.

I padded in, my tail swishing side to side, and rested under his wooden easel.

"How many works did Sir Winston paint?" the journalist asked.

Grace replied, "Well over five hundred. He discovered oils after he resigned from the Admiralty following the Gallipoli fiasco in the Great War in 1915. He had some sketching and drawing talent from his childhood which he polished up a bit at Sandhurst. He created oils like these for almost the next five decades, eventually stopping two years ago."

Someone must have tracked a wet leaf onto the smooth wooden floor. I approached it until I was a suitable distance away then pounced upon it. Then I repeatedly batted it around, jumping up to take another swipe at it with my paws then skidding because of my forward momentum. Great fun!

"Looking at his pictures hung here, I can see he painted landscapes, still lifes, and some portraits."

"That's right," agreed Grace. "He painted harbors, trees, ruins, bridges, sunsets, and even circus elephants. He also painted flowers in vases, fruit, bottles that he called 'bottlescapes,' and views of Chartwell in all seasons. Sir Winston, however, mostly painted landscapes because he concluded, trees didn't complain when he failed to do them justice!"

As I looked over the many canvases that were stacked up to the ceiling, I noticed there weren't any of cats! Why no cats? It was clearly an oversight. He must have his cat portraits somewhere in the main house where he can see them frequently. When I'm inside, I'll have to look for them.

"Did he paint all these here in this studio?" the journalist inquired.

"He mostly painted *en plein air*, that is, outdoors. I think he enjoyed the challenge of working quickly to capture the changing light. Sometimes he'd touch up a larger canvas afterward in here. On a few occasions he worked from a photograph."

Exhausted by my acrobatic gyrations, I settled again under the easel.

"Who influenced his art?"

"Being a prominent member of society, he attracted some capable mentors. These included

Sir John Lavery, Walter Sickert, Paul Maze, and Sir William Nicholson. Sir Winston also liked the works of Turner and the French impressionists."

"Did he ever meet any of the impressionists?"

"They were all gone by the time he took up oils," Grace noted. "Clementine did meet Camille Pissarro once, who essentially was the father of the impressionists."

The journalist walked over to a table that contained neatly stacked tubes of oils. "What were his motivations for his work?"

"I'm sure you read his charming essay and subsequent book, *Painting as a Pastime*. He painted for pleasure and relaxation. It gave him some mental relief from his demanding life in politics. When he painted, his intense artistic focus allowed him to forget all the trials and tribulations taking place around him."

"Then, given all the stresses of being the prime minister, he must have painted a great deal during the Second World War."

"Actually, he only painted once during the entire war. Following a meeting with President Roosevelt in 1943, they drove to Marrakesh where Sir Winston showed FDR the glorious light. After the President left, he stayed and painted a panoramic view of what he saw. Peach walls and mosque towers, the ochre desert, and the purple Atlas Mountains were topped by a sapphire sky in the background. He gave the president the landscape as a gift after it was dry and framed."

"Was that Sir Winston's first visit to Marrakesh?"

"No, he initially went in 1936 after John Lavery suggested that he experience the incredible light there. In total he painted over forty-five canvases in Marrakesh before and after the war. It was by far his favorite venue."

"How do critics rate Sir Winston as an artist?"

"He was regarded as a talented amateur with a skillful hand and a good, selective eye. His paintings reveal he worked decisively, painting thickly with quick, confident brushstrokes. In addition, he preferred bright colors that matched his exuberant personality. Furthermore, he reveled in the beauty and wonder around him that he met with a fearless, childlike curiosity and captured boldly on his canvas."

I moved next to some picture frames stacked up against a table and curled up underneath. My eyes got heavy.

Chapter 26

Dawn of Liberation

THE noise of the studio door shutting woke me up. Grace and the journalist were gone. The lights were off, and I was alone inside. Daylight poured through the windows. I looked inquisitively at the front door. I tried to open its door handle but to no avail. I also pushed it, but it didn't yield. I then walked the entire perimeter inside. There were no other doors or openings where I could leave.

I was trapped inside. A prisoner!

Being an upbeat, positive cat by nature, I was sure Grace would discover I was missing and return. I'd just have to be patient like I am when I'm stalking a prospective meal. Cats are good at being longsuffering.

I had nothing to do but sleep. And since I napped often, I did what came naturally to me. It was warmest just beside the window, so I curled up on the wooden floor there and slept.

I woke and walked around again. I jumped up on a ledge but saw no one. My ears twitched nervously. The windows were all closed tightly.

My tummy growled. Maybe if I dozed, I'd feel less hungry.

I repeated my investigations when I awoke. It was dark outside and darker within. I was hungry and thirsty, too.

Grace must be on her way. I'll be eating soon. My water bowl in the bathroom will be filled with cool, refreshing water, and I'll drink my fill before jumping on Winston's soft bed.

The night passed slowly. I woke on numerous instances and perceived that nothing had changed except the intensity of my hunger.

Winston's painting smock was folded across an easel. I pulled it down and detected a faint aroma of my human. I dragged it over by the entrance and lay down upon it.

As I thought about him, my thoughts cleared. I knew that my freedom would be forthcoming because Winston will send everyone to look for me. I can rely on him! Although impatient for the morning, I slept soundly and had no need for cheering dreams. Facts are better than dreams.

The studio door swung open, and Grace hurried in. So did the daylight! It was morning!

"Jock, you're okay! Thank God!! Winston was worried sick!!!"

She picked me up and held me close as she dashed to the main house. "We were so concerned. We didn't see you at lunch, but you frequently skip that meal."

She got that right. I often have important things to do, like patrolling my domain. I'm conflicted about missing lunch with my companion. Nevertheless, a cat has to keep his sense of aloofness.

"When you didn't show up for dinner, Winston dispatched us to find you. Anthony and I grabbed flashlights and checked the street in front of the house. I dreaded discovering your mutilated body along the side of the road. Thankfully, we didn't find you there."

Grace carried me upward past the orchard to the steps by the terrace lawn.

"We looked all over, by the fish ponds, swimming pool, upper and lower lake fronts, gardens, and rose walk. We were afraid you had been attacked by a fox or owl. We looked through every room in the house but without success."

I'm glad I was missed. It's nice to feel needed!

"We stopped our search close to midnight, vowing to continue at daybreak. Winston was distraught. Roy told me he slept poorly last night. I didn't sleep well either. I tried to think where you might have gone. When I woke, I thought about where I had seen you last—the studio. I got dressed and hurried over here straightaway."

We entered the double front doors to the house. "I found him!" Grace called. "Here he is, safe and sound."

Winston took me from Grace's hands and thrust his face into my neck and shoulder. He then looked up and smiled broadly with tears pouring from his eyes.

I rubbed the sides of my forehead against him and batted his cheek with my paw, purring stridently. It's time to get something to eat and drink!

Chapter 27

If I Lived My Life Again

"HOW much longer do you think I must wait?" Winston asked Anthony as he sat in his basket chair on the terrace lawn. Even though it was a sunny and warm day, the big man in his cowboy hat and heavy coat lay beneath a blanket. I rested under his chair near the back wheels.

Winston was very much an old man in a hurry. Anthony once related to me that Winston was always in a rush, ever since his father died prematurely at the age of forty-five. Winston felt driven because he believed he'd suffer a similar fate. He even thought he would die on the same day, January 24th, that his father did. Fortunately, his private secretary was appropriately diplomatic, ignoring the premonition.

"I read the other day a thought-provoking quotation by Mark Twain. It might appeal to your American side. He said, 'The two most important days in your life are the day you are born and the day you find out why.'"

Cupping a hand around his right ear, Winston listened and pondered the quotation. He then nodded his head and grunted approval. "I met Mark Twain in New York at the turn of the century."

Anthony continued. "I think you as well as the world can identify the answer to the second date. You told me years ago you knew your destiny would involve saving London and England from some disaster."

"I was," Winston recalled, "sixteen years old."

"After you became prime minister in 1940, you were able to fulfill that purpose."

Once again, my human nodded in agreement. Clearing his throat, he asserted, "If I could relive one year of my life, I would choose 1940."

Anthony replied, "You wrote that you felt as if you were walking with destiny, and that all your past life had been but a preparation for that hour and for that trial. Few men in history had such an important destiny. And fewer still were able to accomplish so much for the betterment of mankind."

Anthony's words had a reassuring effect. I think Winston needed reminding that his life had made a difference. Every older person seeks to reconcile his existence and make peace with his achievements.

From my point of view, I did not know the answer to the first date, the day I was born. I had only the fuzziest recollections of my early life. The immediate moment mattered most to me. I bent down over my front paws and stretched before settling again.

A lucky feline is one who finds a gracious benefactor who feeds and cares for him. Winston has done this for me. I have no wants that are unfulfilled. His hands are now gentle. He is compassionate and bighearted, especially with the food he shares with me. The *gruyère* cheese was excellent today! I have cozy and safe places to sleep. I have gardens and outdoor areas to play and hunt. What more could any cat desire?

I am completely dedicated to Winston. I share his life in a way few humans could. My regular presence brings him a sense of comfort when he cannot find fulfillment from his work, hobbies, or interests.

As a cat, my charge now entails being a source of happiness to my human. That undoubtedly is my destiny.

Chapter 28

Blood, Sweat, and Tears

THE weeks of summer flew by. An early autumn colored the trees in reds and rusts, oranges and auburns, yellows and ochres. Winston's life, however, assumed muted hues but not without some of the sparkles that seemed to surround him in kinder years.

Winston and I enjoyed sitting together on the terrace lawn soaking up the sun's rays. He relished the beautiful vistas that unfolded before his eyes. He whispered that this might be his last stay at Chartwell, and he wanted to remember forever the sights he loved. I hoped we'd be back again.

Over a meal of roast shoulder of lamb, both Anthony and Clementine had to speak more loudly so Winston could hear them. After dinner, my human, with Clementine and Anthony, listened to the record player in the drawing room. He had been given an album with recordings of his greatest orations. They were entranced by my human's heroic words.

Emanating from the phonograph, the big man's rich, resonant voice filled the room. I sat on his lap and took short naps during most of the great speechifying. I can still process sounds while I'm catnapping and will become alert if I hear something interesting.

"I would say to the House, as I have said to those who have joined this Government: 'I have nothing to offer but blood, toil, tears, and sweat.'... You ask, what is our policy? I can say: It is to wage war, by sea, land, and air, with all our might and with all the strength that God can give us; to wage war against a monstrous tyranny, never surpassed in the dark lamentable catalogue of human crime. That is our policy. You ask, what is our aim? I can answer in one word: It is victory, victory at all costs, victory in spite of all terror, victory, however long and hard the road may be; for without victory, there is no survival."

Winston mouthed the words and seemed to take immense satisfaction from hearing himself. Then they listened to another of his rousing speeches.

"We shall go on to the end. We shall fight in France, we shall fight on the seas and oceans, we shall fight with growing confidence and growing strength in the air, we shall defend our Island, whatever the cost may be, we shall fight on the beaches, we shall fight on the landing grounds, we shall fight in the fields and in the streets, we shall fight in the hills; we shall never surrender."

Winston puffed out his chest and held his head high. He held his unlighted cigar at a jaunty angle between his lips. His blue eyes blazed with pride. My nose twitched, and I ran my right paw against my vibs.

Anthony selected an album of Gilbert and Sullivan patter songs and placed a record on the turntable.

"When I was a lad I served a term
As office boy to an Attorney's firm.
I cleaned the windows and I swept the
floor,
And I polished up the handle of the big
front door.
(He polished up the handle of the big
front door.)
I polished up that handle so carefully
That now I am the Ruler of the Queen's
Navee!
(He polished up that handle so carefully,
That now he is the ruler of the Queen's
Navee!)"

In his soft, light voice Winston sang all the verses. He tapped his foot in perfect unison with

the music, causing me to bounce up and down on
his lap as if I were in a small boat on a choppy lake.

> "I grew so rich that I was sent
> By a pocket borough into Parliament.
> I always voted at my party's call,
> And I never thought of thinking for
> myself at all.
> (He never thought of thinking for
> himself at all.)
> I thought so little, they rewarded me
> By making me the Ruler of the Queen's
> Navee!
> (He thought so little, they rewarded he
> By making him the Ruler of the Queen's
> Navee!)
>
> Now landsmen all, whoever you may be,
> If you want to rise to the top of the tree,
> If your soul isn't fettered to an office
> stool,
> Be careful to be guided by this golden
> rule.
> (Be careful to be guided by this golden
> rule.)
> Stick close to your desks and never go to
> sea,
> And you all may be rulers of the Queen's
> Navee!
> (Stick close to your desks and never go to
> sea,

And you all may be rulers of the Queen's
Navee!)"

They subsequently listened to some
inspiring military marches followed by melodic
Broadway tunes. Finally they ended with favorite
songs Winston sang when he attended Harrow
School in his youth.

"And two that I know, but may not say,
But we are a pitiful race of clay,
And never will score again.
For all of we,
Whoever we be,
Come short of the giants of old, you
see...

"But I think all this is a lie, you know,
I think all this is a lie;
For the hero-race may come and go,
But it doesn't exactly die!
For the match we lose and win it again,
And a Balliol comes to us now and then,

"And if we are dwarfing in bat and pen,
Down to the last of the Harrow men,
We will know the reason why!
For all of we,
Whoever we be,
Come up to the giants of old, you see."

My human glowed with a healthy color as he finished singing these beloved tunes. What a stirring way to end his final night at Chartwell! Tomorrow we'd caravan to his London home for the wintertime.

I walked up the stairs and joined him as Roy pushed him in his wheelchair from the lift, a gift from Max Beaverbrook eons ago. I jumped onto his bed and waited for Winston to join me. He fell asleep immediately, as always, his heart full, as was mine.

Winston and Clementine were relaxed and serene as they sat together on the couch in the drawing room while waiting for their baggage to be loaded in the cars for the trip back to London.

The daylight oozed in through the garden windows, giving a sensation of airy, lush brightness. Fresh-cut flowers filled the room with an alluring scent.

I sat on my human's lap. My eyes were heavy as I fought the drowsiness that would soon overcome me. My tail moved lazily as the two spoke in quiet tones. Hers were words, and his were more like indistinct sounds of understanding.

Clementine smiled at her husband with great affection in her eyes. Her curly white hair contrasted with his almost complete lack of hair. She reached out with a dainty hand and touched his.

Looking at me then at her husband, she said, "You really love him, don't you?"

Winston smiled too, and I could see tears glistening in his blue eyes. He didn't need to nod because she already knew what his reply would be.

I purred softly as she spoke again. "At first, I had my doubts about Jock," she paused, "but I now regard him as an extraordinary cat, thoroughly devoted to you. In fact, I think there should always be a Jock here at Chartwell, don't you?"

This time he bowed his head in agreement. His hand stroked my back, his touch comforting and reassuring. Then the two sat in companionable silence.

My eyes closed as I drifted off to slumber, happy and content on Winston's lap.

Chapter 29

Their Finest Hour

I reacquainted myself with my feline friends upon returning to our London home. We exchanged scents. Being the dominant cat now, I led by example and pestered the terrier.

The weather turned decidedly cooler, and my winter coat came in. I'd been pawing at my right ear for a few days. Whenever anyone touched me there, I moved my head away as the pain throbbed. The vet was called.

The vet diagnosed an ear infection and prescribed an ointment which he administered after grabbing me in the bathroom. That was a cheap shot. I was lured in with the promise of a piece of cheese only to be trapped when he slid the door closed. I resisted him with all my skill and cunning, but his practiced hands prevailed.

After being dosed and the door opened, I leaped free from him and disappeared under the bed. I shook my head forcefully as my heart beat fast. Like the big man, I'm an uncooperative patient.

When I heard the vet exit the study, I warily peeked out from under the bed. Happily, the coast was clear, so I jumped up on the bed and took a nap next to Winston.

After we woke, he looked over at me.

"Jock, we're alike in many ways."

My tail swayed easily in broad sweeps with its tip curling and uncurling.

"You're ginger in color. When I was a young subaltern, my hair was ginger-colored, too."

I blinked my eyes slowly not because of what he said but because of the affectionate way he said it. Cats are passionate creatures especially to those we love.

We've had some rain but so far, no snow. Winston spends hours in the drawing room and has become especially quiet and withdrawn. Clementine, Anthony, Mary, and Roy all try to engage him. Now the occasional visitor has to carry on a mostly one-sided conversation.

Jock Colville came by one afternoon. In a loud voice, so Winston could hear him, he said, "Winston, I'm happy to see you. And you, too, Mr. Cat."

I sat on my human's lap adding further warmth. My namesake reminded Winston of what a privilege it was serving as his private secretary during both of his premierships, the first tour being cut short when he transferred to the RAF for three years during the war. Later he returned to his secretarial post. Winston listened intently, occasionally nodding his head.

"We were separated in age by four decades," Mr. Jock mentioned, "when I first joined you. Because I previously worked for Neville Chamberlain, I had my reservations about you. Also you were sixty-five years of age when you became prime minister in 1940, and some were not sure you'd be up to the demands of a wartime leader. But all that changed rapidly as you took the reins of government and mobilized us against the Nazi threat. I can't think of another man who could have borne the burdens you endured for five long years of grueling war!"

Winston frowned and leaned forward. Mr. Jock understood and spoke a little louder.

"Winston, I'm not sure you fully recognize what a singular debt not only all Englishmen, but the entire western world, owe you. Your leadership was characterized by three elements: uncanny vision, undaunted courage, and unconquerable determination. Your drive, decisions, and diplomacy transformed you into a premier statesman, a preeminent war leader, and a dedicated peacemaker.

"But I wanted to look beyond your many deeds to your character, which became the true legacy you gave us all."

Mr. Jock was giving Winston a pep talk, one that he badly needed to hear.

"No leader was ever so magnanimous to the fallen adversary as you were. All your life you have shown that quality to those who failed to triumph over your indomitable will, be they political opponents or vanquished enemies."

In a low voice, Winston replied, "Generosity is always wise."

"Exactly!" beamed Mr. Jock. "The moral you used for your magnificent war memoir captured the essence of who you have been: 'In War—Resolution, In Defeat—Defiance, In Victory—Magnanimity, In Peace—Goodwill.'

"This harks back to who you are as a man and as a leader of men. Your achievements are so many and so significant. Over sixty years in Parliament and over fourteen years in uniform. Serving six sovereigns. Your books, articles, letters, and memos. Your speeches. Millions of words. The Nobel Prize for Literature. Your leadership and administration of eleven different

Cabinet ministries including serving twice as prime minister during critical epochs in our history.

"Your glory is enshrined forever, Winston! You have reached this unique pinnacle of human achievement.

"In addition you have always been a constitutionalist, believing that government exists to serve man and not the other way around. You stood for the undeniable freedom of every man and woman to live their lives unfettered by the force, domination, and tyranny of evil. You also embraced liberty, bathed in the clean, pure light of truth, justice, and equality."

I looked into my human's face. A slight smile crossed his tired face. In earlier years he might have replied with equal force, conviction, and enthusiasm. Winston had been an optimist; the brandy glass was always half full. Now his body was exhausted, and his mind had difficulty focusing for too long on any one subject.

Somewhere deep inside this complex man the words formed. With humility and gratitude Winston replied with heartfelt simplicity, "Thank you, Jock, my dear friend."

In one sentence, perhaps he had acknowledged both of us.

Chapter 30

Victory

HUGE crowds gathered in front of Winston's home the day before his ninetieth birthday. They filled the area outside the front windows as well as the cul-de-sac just beyond the second townhouse. They didn't want to miss the opportunity to see the greatest living Englishman.

Roy dressed Winston in his comfortable green velvet siren suit. Surprisingly, it didn't show my fur as badly as his darker siren suits. After Clementine made sure her husband looked his best, he carefully walked over to the front window. Because he was unsteady on his feet, both Clementine and an attendant were standing nearby to assist him if he needed it.

The crowd went wild when they saw him.

"Good ol' Winnie!" they shouted. "For he's a jolly good fellow." Then they sang happy birthday to him. Musicians serenaded him, and the crowd applauded him.

Winston smiled, waved, and flashed his famous V-for-victory sign. That was what the crowd wanted to see. Their love and affection for the big man were palpable. The individuals in the crowd were eager to witness this living legend and hero so that they might someday tell their children, grandchildren, and friends that they had seen him with their own eyes.

I stood next to him, but even by standing on my hind legs, my head barely reached the bottom of the window. As he withdrew from the tumultuous display, I could see tears in his eyes.

He was touched by the enthusiastic affection his countrymen had shown him. A leader wants to feel both needed and loved, and Winston was no exception. I felt the same way about him, but my displays of warmth entailed rubbing the sides of my forehead against his face.

My human fed me some of his roast beef, cooked rare, during lunch. It always tasted better coming from his fingers than when I gulped food out of my own bowl. Afterward I sat on his lap while he watched an American television show, "Sea Hunt." I think if the big man were as young as the actor, Lloyd Bridges, he, too, might have taken up scuba diving the same way Grace said he took up flying when aircraft were primitive affairs.

After a late afternoon nap, he had an early dinner. The piece of fresh Scottish salmon he shared with me really hit the spot. He then watched a special, star-studded birthday tribute to him on the BBC. Clementine and Sarah watched the show with him. Both Winston and his daughter were captivated by the music and tapped their feet to the tunes. I swayed my tail but not to any particular melody.

I followed Winston to bed and jumped up after he settled under the covers. His hand reached over and stroked me down my back. I lay completely still but purred noisily. I was the luckiest cat alive! As usual, he fell asleep immediately.

The next morning, Roy opened the drapes to let the bright morning light shine in. He wished his charge many happy returns on this his ninetieth birthday.

For breakfast, he had his usual coffee with cream but apricot jam on his toast instead of his customary black cherry. I preferred the black cherry. He read several newspapers, paying particular attention to stories about him. They even had a front-page picture of him in the window waving.

Anthony gave Winston a framed photo of me that Monty had taken, and the big man kept it near his bed. I was touched.

After kissing her husband on the forehead, Clementine sang happy birthday to him.

Housemaids carried in flowers from well-wishers, including the Queen. Telegrams and birthday cards flooded in. I heard Anthony mention that over 70,000 telegrams, messages, cards, and presents had arrived.

Winston had lunch in bed to sustain his strength for the upcoming dinner party. Clementine and Anthony joined him. I dined with him as usual. The lamb cutlets were delicious. I never miss an opportunity to enjoy "people food." Frankly, I'm spoiled, but fortunately all my activity prevents me from turning into a fat cat.

Large crowds had gathered again, hoping to catch a glimpse of the great man. Winston did not deny them, walking to the window to acknowledge their cheers.

The butler announced Prime Minister Harold Wilson, who visited in mid-afternoon with well wishes from the Cabinet.

Nearby in the townhouse office, six secretaries sorted bags of mail and telegrams. They brought over the more important ones, and Anthony dictated appropriate replies. I think the big man relished feeling important again. All the activity energized him rather than depleting his much-reduced reserves.

Winston made a grand entrance into the dining room unaided, waving away Randolph's assistance. The family all stood and applauded. Winston took the cigar from his mouth, held it up jauntily, and returned the smiles with a broad one of his own.

Clementine, Randolph, Sarah, Mary, young Winston, Anthony, and a dozen others surrounded the birthday boy. I heard someone say Monty was in the hospital and unable to attend. Randolph seemed in a festive mood and made no attempt to shoo me off.

Mr. Jock gave me a congenial head tap.

"Mr. Cat, it's been two years since I rescued you and brought you to Winston," he said. "You've become a valued member of his family."

With my tail held high, I rubbed my body alongside his legs.

While the happy family and friends dined by candlelight on oysters, partridge, fruit, cheese, and ice cream, my human made sure I had a nice tin of tuna.

Winston tried to lift himself up to make a speech but was dissuaded from doing so. Instead Randolph said some appropriate words—devoid of his usual hostility—and everyone raised a glass of champagne to their father, husband, or friend.

Winston was thoroughly exhausted when the last guests departed. After I heard all the noise and activity subside, I went into the drawing room where I found Winston sitting alone next to the fire. Replete with good food, good conversations, good cheer, and much love, his cup runneth over. We watched the last logs burn down with a simmering hiss before slowly proceeding to his bedroom.

Winston's blue slippers sat on the carpet next to his bed. I batted one with a paw and then grabbed it with my teeth and front paws. I then brought up my rear paws attacking it and rolling around with it on the floor. The big man rested on the edge of his bed and reached for it. I pulled it beyond his reach. He simply sat there and smiled.

Today was a significant milestone for Winston, his family, and his country. His promise to his people on that somber day in 1940 was that their collective aim was victory. The adulation he had received this afternoon reminded him of when he spoke from the balcony of the Ministry of Health on VE Day almost twenty years earlier. "This is your victory," he had told the jubilant throngs. And they had shouted back, "No, it's yours."

Nothing was so uplifting to the ninety-year-old hero of his nation as having his countrymen honor him on his birthday.

Chapter 31

The Gathering Storm

LIKE the aftermath of a great battle, the post-birthday period was anticlimactic. My human was unusually quiet. Fortuitously, I was there with him. And he responded by stroking behind my ears while I purred in appreciation, hopefully with enough force for him to hear or feel me.

The sky was dark with ominous rain clouds. A noisy bird outdoors caught my attention one morning while Winston was eating breakfast. I immediately jumped atop a table to get a better view. I grew more and more excited as the bird happily chirped, but I was frustrated because the window separated me from my prey. I chattered so urgently that Winston put down his toast and watched me. Unfortunately, my theatrics could not dispel the gloom that had descended on him.

His inactivity found him vacantly watching the ever-burning blaze in the fireplace. Neither book nor newspaper could occupy his mind. He slept more and engaged with people less. His moments of mirth or wit were much less frequent, too.

To elicit a reaction from him, I climbed atop his chest and kneaded him with my front paws, my upright tail nearest his chin. He would typically turn me around, so we were face-to-face. This is what I wanted him to do, but it didn't work. I also tried to tickle his chin with my vibs. I thought if I could just get him moving, he'd be more spirited, but it was not to be.

A bleak winter nestled around us. The big man watched television, especially on Sunday afternoons when adventure programs were broadcast. For fleeting instants, he was transported into places removed in time and space from his current humdrum existence.

In his earlier days my human had been a man of action, a perpetual motion machine. He met or exceeded every demand that was placed upon him. Now he struggled with even the simplest endeavors of his daily existence.

Winston had to summon special reserves to attend a lunch at the Other Club in the Pinafore Room at the Savoy Hotel, a bittersweet experience since all his oldest friends were gone.

It was cold and frosty on Christmas Day. My human was definitely not in the Christmas spirit. He walked sluggishly and needed much help from his nurses. His breathing seemed labored, as if any exertion were too much for him. He spoke little. Occasionally he felt chilled even in the heated drawing room.

He ate slowly, consuming only small amounts. Frequently he had to be fed, but he still shared tidbits with me. His hands remained gentle and caring although they seemed to shake more. I purred loudly to let him know I appreciated his kindness.

I pursued what smells I could find in the bleak garden. It was too cold for Winston to sit outdoors, so he watched me from the windows in his bedroom. Not long after Christmas, he caught a mild chill, and a cold soon developed. A doctor was called, but fortunately, his condition improved.

I lay beside him on his bed. He was reclining on several pillows and gazing up at the ceiling. I felt an overwhelming warmth flood through my body. This man had taken me into his home and shared his life with me.

I made little meows as I rubbed the sides of my forehead against his face. I felt his lavender-scented hands reach over my back to caress it.

New Year's Day no longer held a magic promise of new opportunities. It passed quietly without special notice or celebration.

One night, just after Winston climbed into bed, he confessed some very personal thoughts to me. Instead of quickly falling into slumber like he usually did, he talked in a slow, halting, and subdued voice.

"Jock, I look forward to dying. Sleep, endless, wonderful sleep."

I sensed the tension in the air and responded in the only way I could, with my presence. I stretched my body alongside his. I felt his body relax, and he began to snore.

Winston was always most joyful at Chartwell. The air and beautiful vistas renewed his spirit. Now the dreariness of a London winter had invaded his heart. He seemed resigned to whatever would come, a radical departure from a man who was always vigorous and wanted to be in control of his life.

The next week he dined with Clementine as his only human guest. He shared some of his cold duck with me. Delicious, of course. He indulged in his usual libations, champagne and brandy. His cigar remained between his lips but unlit.

Afterward in the drawing room, Anthony joined us. As they watched the flames dance, Winston said, "Old age is intolerable." He ruminated on this a while longer then continued, "Time used to be an ally but no longer."

Anthony sensed that Winston was perhaps reexperiencing what occurred when the gathering storm clouds in Europe were about to unleash their fury. In this case, however, it was the calm before the storm on a personal scale.

Chapter 32

The Hinge of Fate

WINSTON had difficulty sleeping, which was unusual for him. During his terribly restless and fitful night, I could tell that not only was he breathing more slowly than he normally did, but that his heart was beating more irregularly. He remained in bed all the next day, rising only for dinner. He was quiet and more downcast.

He even refused the cigar and brandy Roy offered him, an alarming sign. Furthermore, he was unwilling to go to bed afterward. When he at last climbed in, I hopped next to him, but he didn't seem to recognize that I was beside him. In addition, his eyes seemed to be darting around.

The next morning his doctor examined him. Winston was listless and uninterested in food. I had my normal appetite and rubbed up against a housemaid's leg until she deciphered my intentions and fed me. Another doctor, unfamiliar to me, came in and examined him. He and the regular doctor conferred where even I could not hear them.

Clementine ordered bouquets of colorful, fragrant flowers to decorate her husband's bedroom. Lavender wasn't blooming then, but flowers were brought in which resembled those that decorated Chartwell. These failed to rouse him.

Randolph, Mary, and young Winston stopped by. When I saw Randolph, I resolved to hold my ground and stay on the bed next to my sleeping companion. My ears became fully flattened over my head as if I were putting on my battle helmet to protect me from impending combat. I was prepared to hiss if he tried to shoo me off the bed. I was completely astonished when he actually laid his hand on my back and gently rubbed me. I made a small noise of approval in my throat.

What had caused this change of attitude? Perhaps I had misjudged him.

Winston's face had a grayish cast. In case the heavy blanket, quilt, and three radiators weren't enough to keep him warm, I added my body to the layers that enveloped him. That evening the room was lit only by a green night-light which gave an ominous glow to the surroundings.

In the morning the two doctors returned, examined him again, and conferred with

Clementine. I looked through the open door and saw her bring her hands to her face in distress. While waiting for my food bowl, I heard the nurse say that my human had suffered a massive stroke, but surely two doctors could help him twice as much.

The next morning Winston opened his eyes, but they had an empty look to them. I sat next to him, my ears rotated forward, alert, observing him intently. The full-length flowered curtains that covered the bay windows were opened, allowing the veiled light from the garden to cover the room. He had difficulty moving his left hand, and his ability to focus was gone. He didn't seem to recognize anyone.

When he was dozing, I noticed his right hand opening and closing. Then it moved forward and back. Was he smoking an unseen cigar? Was he gesturing during a speech? Was he painting in his sleep? Perhaps he was summoning me to join him on his basket chair on the terrace lawn.

Mary's husband, Christopher, offered Winston a glass of champagne, but he refused, stating, "I'm so bored with it all." The family thought these were Winston's last words. I didn't. The big man always had at least a little more to say.

He now coughed with a bad rasping sound. His eyes remained closed. He had few periods of wakefulness. However, I did not abandon my post. I wanted to be there when he woke.

Clementine and Mary sat with him as he lay unresponsive in his bed. They watched without words as his chest rose and fell beneath the blanket, a reassurance for them both.

Meanwhile, Roy, thoroughly exhausted by his constant vigilance, was aided by two day nurses and two night nurses.

I maintained my vigil around the clock, only leaving when I was hungry or needed to answer the call of nature. Nurses or family members moistened the big man's lips with water. Young Winston often stopped by nightly to sit with him.

The next day was cold and gray. His condition had not changed. The press and concerned well-wishers flooded the street in front of the townhomes and nearby cul-de-sac. By now the world knew he was ill, but I trusted that he'd pull through, as he always did. I resolved to be patient.

Some days passed, and Winston suddenly seemed to be getting a little better. He was breathing easier. His color looked better, too, without the bluish tint he'd previously had. His elevated temperature fell.

The Sergeant, Winston's devoted protector, who was standing watch in front of the townhouse, came inside. He grasped the big man's hand and was surprised when Winston gripped him back. The bodyguard then patted me on my head. He was always kind to me. As he departed, I saw tears in his eyes.

After a short while, young Winston stood noiselessly in the bedroom and just observed his grandfather. Then he spoke softly to him. He was concerned that his grandfather was not getting enough to drink and that he might be thirsty.

Winston's lips did appear dry, and they seemed to move as if he were requesting water. Actually, he probably wanted champagne or cognac! Nonetheless, his dutiful grandson poured a tiny glass of orange juice from the nearby carafe. Contrary to the doctor's orders, he gave him a small sip.

Late in the night I sensed my human stir. His hand moved slowly over my back. Then I felt his familiar fingers squeeze me ever so slightly. His voice was but a whisper. "Jock, my cat," he said. He was silent for a moment then continued, "I knew you'd be ..." He stopped again then finished with, "here." I treasured his words and purred intensely to let him know I heard him.

Chapter 33

Triumph and Tragedy

IN the morning Winston's condition took a turn for the worse. His breathing became scratchy and erratic, and his heart continued to beat weakly. Family and intimate friends arrived and departed. Their hushed whispers spoke of their concern.

More days passed with no change except for fresh flowers. There were no meals in the dining room and no visitors in the drawing room. Unless the big man woke briefly while I had been outside or eating in the kitchen, this was his longest sleep.

As Winston slept, his delicate hands rested on the white quilt pulled up to his chin. His head was propped up by several pillows to help him breathe more easily.

I curled up beside him, determined to be there when his eyes opened. Roy did not chase me away.

One of the nurses said Winston had had a long, adventure-filled life. He was reliving his memories and needed time to visit them all. This mean nothing to me since my human often slept soundly.

Day and night merged into one long seamless event. Winston's personal doctor arrived and briefly examined his patient. Was having only one doctor a good sign? Or a bad one because he stopped by every day? Clementine and Mary sat with him, taking turns holding his hand. Sarah and a granddaughter also visited Winston daily as he slept. Once Randolph stopped by, lifted up his father's hand to his lips, and kissed it—unusual behavior for him.

Clementine always came in to say good-night before she turned in. If she woke in the middle of the night, she invariably made her way to her husband's bedroom to check on him, her face a mask of concern. She didn't seem surprised by my presence.

One evening I heard Clementine proudly announce that their granddaughter-in-law had given birth to a baby boy. She had been resting, so Randolph had left her a brief note with the good news. This ray of sunlight broke through the gloom of the darkened bedroom.

The lifted spirits faded two days later on a gloomy, overcast morning, when the entire family, Roy, Anthony, the doctor, and a few others gathered in the lamplit bedchamber. Why so many visitors when the big man was still sleeping? And they did not speak, even to each other.

The clock in the drawing room had just chimed eight times. All watched the small, still figure of my human cloaked in blankets and comforter. I lay on the bed by the lower part of his legs. Most did not seem to notice me. Those that did touched my back or head, but I was reluctant to purr in the quiet room.

Clementine, on Winston's right, refused to release his hand. I raised my head and looked into the solemn faces of Mary, Sarah, and a granddaughter, all of whom were kneeling at the foot of the bed. Young Winston, with Randolph standing behind him, stood to Winston's left, their faces somber. Others at the back of the room had fallen to their knees. This frightened me, although I didn't know why.

Time froze in the dimly lit room. Everyone listened and waited. Then Winston gave two or three barely audible sighs and was still.

Clementine looked over at the doctor who nodded slowly. The humans stayed for a while, unspeaking. Then individually they stood up and quietly departed. This disturbed me. Should I leave? No one said so, but I felt uneasy. I finally hopped off the bed and climbed the stairs to the second floor. I found an open room, went inside, and hid under a bed.

People came and went in the house during the rest of that day and into the next. I was neither hungry nor felt a need to go outdoors. Late in the afternoon as I sat on the steps, I heard his voice.

At first, I thought I might be dreaming. But there it was! It was unmistakable! With resonance, power, and passion, it grew in intensity. I was running now, running toward the sound of my human. He was awake and stronger than ever! I couldn't wait to jump into his arms and rub my head against his face!

"Let us therefore brace ourselves to our duties, and so bear ourselves that, if the British Empire and its Commonwealth last for a thousand years, men will still say, 'This was their finest hour.'"

With joy in my heart, I sprinted through the open door of Winston's bedroom, expecting to see him sitting up, smiling, his cigar in hand. But I leaped onto an empty bed, the darkened room surrounded by flickering candles. He wasn't lying there any longer. Why not?

Just off the foot of the bed sat a strange, elevated box. I walked over to it. Winston was lying inside the box. This couldn't be comfortable. And he was wearing a formal, three-piece suit and his favorite blue bowtie with white polka dots. I gaped at him briefly before nimbly jumping and landing on his body, then walking across his chest.

He wasn't moving or breathing. I looked down at his still, white face. All his deeply-etched wrinkles and facial tension were gone. He looked serene, indeed peaceful.

I tried to wake him by kneading on his chest and rubbing my forehead against his cold cheek. Where were his blankets when he needed them the most? I uttered short, insistent meows, but nothing broke the trance he was in.

I sniffed. He no longer had the aura. I moved in closer and sniffed again. No scent of lavender or even cigar smoke. The man I once knew was gone. This must be what Winston had called the black velvet of eternal sleep, a complete separation from the present.

I yowled with pain, extending my body, so I was lying across my human's chest with my head up to his chin.

I suddenly realized Winston Churchill had saved my life, but in the end, I was unable to save his.

He had been without a pet and was lonesome. I was in danger. Mr. Jock felt compassion for his friend and thus solved two problems simultaneously, Winston's and mine.

I grew to love Winston, and I know he loved me. We kept each other company and formed an endearing bond. The memory of our togetherness, the meals, the gardens, the homes, and the games all flashed across my mind. What fun we had together!

My fur time with him brought us both solace. He confided some of his most closely-held thoughts to me. I reciprocated with deep purrs, head nudges, kneading, and chest warmings.

I miss my human already! My world has been turned upside down! I've lost the most important person to me, and I'm devastated! Never again will I feel his comforting touch or hear his kind, gentle voice!

I struggle to breathe as the enormity of this loss engulfs me with sadness, and I'm so overwhelmed with this new situation that I'm not sure what to do next. I feel empty and numb as the light and color of my life seem to have bled into shades of darkness. Winston is no longer here, and I am alone.

Then a faint sound startled me. Turning, I saw Anthony watching me from the doorway. I cannot face any humans right now. The only one I truly care about, Winston, is gone. I leaped out of the box onto his bed, then out of his bedroom, never to return.

In the hall, a radio continued to broadcast a news report of Winston Churchill's death.

Epilogue

JOCK was Sir Winston Leonard Spencer Churchill's last cat. He was rescued from the RSCPA by John Rupert (Jock) Colville, Churchill's private secretary during his two premierships and later a close family friend (who was knighted in 1974). He gave the kitten to Churchill for his eighty-eighth birthday on 30 November 1962.

Jock the cat survived being hit by a car on the road that fronted Chartwell as well as a bout with pneumonia. He enjoyed meals with Sir Winston and slept first in the hall outside his bedroom and afterward on his bed. He sat on Churchill's lap during the group photo of his grandson's wedding reception and was seen at Churchill's feet while he waved to the crowd from the front of his London home. Near the end of his life, Churchill kept a photo of Jock by his bed.

During Churchill's final days, Jock was ever faithful to his human, remaining on his bed until he passed away on 24 January 1965, exactly seventy years to the day after his father's death. According to Sir Anthony Arthur Duncan

Montague Browne, Churchill's last private secretary, Jock inspected Churchill's still body in his open coffin.

After her husband's death, Clementine Churchill sold #27 and #28 Hyde Park Gate and took a smaller residence nearby. Chartwell reverted on Churchill's death to the National Trust, where it was restored to the floor plan it had when the Churchills lived there in the 1930s. Grace Hamblin, Clementine's private secretary, became the first administrator of Chartwell. In 1966 it was opened to the public.

Jock moved back to Chartwell after Churchill's death and lived his remaining days there, relishing the gardens, fields, woods, and ponds. He grieved for the loss of his friend during that first year without Winston, but eventually the country estate worked its magic on him and ministered to his sorrow. He and Grace enjoyed many fine moments together in the ensuing nine years.

Jock passed away late in 1974 at the age of twelve and was buried in the Chartwell pet graveyard next to Churchill's poodles, Rufus and Rufus II. A stone marks his grave with his name, Jock, and the dates 1962-74 etched in the stone.

Clementine's promise to her husband that there should always be a Jock at Chartwell has been honored. As of this writing, Jock VI is the current resident cat. Visitors often see the marmalade cat with the white bib and socks patrolling his domain in much the same way as the original Jock.

Acknowledgements

I discovered Winston Churchill on the day he died, Sunday, 24 January 1965. I was fifteen and have studied his life and leadership ever since. Three years into my journey, I read about Jock for the first time.

Churchill's Cat: A Feline Remembrance has been exhaustively researched over the past six years using primary sources by individuals who were actually there. The events, locations, and people described are historically accurate. Jock's thoughts are of course, Jock's. Any errors of interpretation are by definition, his and mine.

Mittens, a black-and-white tuxedo cat, was my first moggy in 1989, followed by Maggie, a trim calico who lived to be nineteen; Muffie, a sweet but overweight calico; Dixie, an affectionate black-and-silver tabby; Toby, an outgoing all black cat; Big Ben, a friendly nineteen-pound marmalade tabby; and my current cat, Clemmie, a loving black-and- brown tabby, now eight. All my cats have been strays who adopted us. These wonderful, playful, responsive creatures helped me to understand cat behavior. In addition, I closely collaborated with Clemmie during the writing of this book.

Ever since I learned about Jock, I thought it would make an entertaining story. It was not long after I visited Chartwell in 2013 that I believed it was opportune to write a book concerning this amazing cat. Later, after standing in front of #27 and #28 Hyde Park Gate in 2016, I realized that the setting for the book would revolve around Churchill's two homes in London and Kent.

My preceding book, *CHURCHILL Without Blood, Sweat, or Tears: Applying His Methods for Today's Leaders*, completed on 30 November 2017, was an attempt to identify Churchill's leadership strategy in a way that was readily understandable to business people and ordinary citizens. This book pinpoints the personal traits that made Churchill the extraordinary person he was.

There are a number of hints in this work that hark back to Churchill's life, wit, candor, and eloquence. For example, all the chapter titles in *Churchill's Cat* were taken from titles of books, articles, or speeches by Winston Churchill. While the non-Churchillian reader may not realize these nuances, I hope my fellow Churchillians will enjoy them.

In a surprising coincidence, two of Churchill's oldest acquaintances also passed away with their devoted cats on their deathbeds: Professor Frederick Alexander ("the Prof") Lindemann, the 1st Viscount Cherwell, his good friend and advisor, and Sir Edward Howard (Eddie) Marsh, Churchill's first private secretary (1905-15, 1916-22, and 1924-29).

As with my four previous books, I have been blessed by the contributions of many generous, knowledgeable, and conscientious friends. Some contributed countless hours while others offered a word of encouragement at just the right moment. Without their dedicated help, this book would not be possible.

I sincerely appreciate the invaluable assistance from: Cita Stelzer, Dr. Piers Brendon, Dr. Allen Packwood, Cheryl Servais, Richard Langworth, Dulany Howland and his wife Vicki, David Riddle, Heather Gregory, Randolph Spencer Churchill and his wife Catherine, Katherine Barnett Carter, Lee Pollock, Kevin Degenhard (RSPCA), Julie Knight (RSPCA), Dr. David Freeman, Nanette Towsley, John Henry King, CDR Bruce Wolven (CANOA), Thomas F. Gede, Paul Kryske, Julie Tabor, Jeff Gottlieb, Tom Kryske, Lisa Albuquerque, Master Chief Musician Jay Piper, Joni McPherson, Jane Davies,

Dr. Chris Terrill, Chuck Apthorp, Gene Wismer, Paul Gottlieb, Kyle Kryske, and CAPT W. Dallas Bethea (CANOA).

The International Churchill Society has exposed me to kindred spirits, Churchillians, many of whom have become stalwart friends. Their quarterly journal, *Finest Hour*, is a superior resource about all things Churchill. The depth of material and the quality of its presentation are quite remarkable. ICS also has an incredible website at WinstonChurchill.org.

Hillsdale College's Churchill Project is another splendid resource. Not only are they completing the companion volumes to Sir Martin Gilbert's official biography, but they have a treasure trove of scholarly articles about Churchill. These can be found at WinstonChurchill.Hillsdale.edu.

The National Trust oversees Chartwell. Churchill used to say, "A day away from Chartwell is a day wasted." The National Trust is to be applauded for their dedicated efforts in preserving and protecting the English heritage by making this national treasure available to the public. Their website is: NationalTrust.org.uk/Chartwell.

My dad, Leon, who passed away last year at 91.5 years of age, gave me many insights into Churchill's physical condition during his final years. I'm sure he and my mom, Annette, who preceded him in death by nine months at the age of almost 90, would have enjoyed this book.

And in the spirit that the last shall be first, my wife, Naomi, an extremely talented and serious novelist in her own right, has generously helped me with every facet of this book. Hers was a labor of love for which I'm truly grateful. Her life-changing novels, *The Witness*, *The Mission*, and the completion of the trilogy currently in writing, *The Hostage*, have become for me the gold standard in how to develop unforgettable characters, advance compelling plots, and "show, don't tell."

About the Author

COMMANDER Lawrence Michael (Larry) Kryske, United States Navy (Ret.) develops victorious leaders who have vision, courage, and determination. He is an author, professional speaker, certified trainer, and facilitator who has over forty-five years of worldwide success leading men and women and building unstoppable teams.

As a career naval officer, Larry served in warships in the U.S. Pacific Fleet including two guided missile destroyers, a fleet frigate, and a guided missile cruiser. He was involved in combat operations during the Vietnam War in his first ship and deployment in the Persian Gulf war zone on his fourth ship, where he qualified for command at sea.

He served ashore in Naval Intelligence in Japan, on the Chief of Naval Operations' staff in the Pentagon, and with the Defense Nuclear Agency. Larry was also the first commanding officer of U.S. Naval Station, Pascagoula, Mississippi, which was the Navy's newest, most sophisticated, technologically modern, and environmentally clean base.

He went on to serve as a private school administrator and instructor, teaching courses on leadership for high school students at two schools (as well as teaching regular and AP courses on U.S. and world history, geography, art, and public speaking at the second school).

Larry is president of Your Finest Hour Leadership Programs, a full-service leadership development business that started in 1996. He speaks nationwide on leadership, teamwork, and innovation. He has given keynotes, conducted training seminars, and facilitated leadership retreats for over 100,000 individuals in four hundred corporate, non-profit (trade associations), governmental, educational, and civic organizations in over fifty different industries.

Larry is a respected authority on the life and leadership of Winston Churchill. He served a three-year term on the Board of Directors of the International Churchill Society.

Larry authored four previous books about how to apply Churchill's leadership today and is a landscape oil painter. He gave his painting keynote presentation, Creating Your Finest Hour, about Churchill's leadership strategy, to over 50,000 people throughout the United States and Canada.

Larry has a BA in Astronomy from the University of California at Los Angeles (UCLA), where he also rowed on UCLA's crew, and an MS in Applied Science from the Naval Postgraduate School in Monterey, CA. He resides in Plano, Texas, with his wife, Naomi, a crime/suspense novelist.

Contact Larry at:
Larry@YourFinestHour.com

CPSIA information can be obtained
at www.ICGtesting.com
Printed in the USA
LVHW090606280819
628924LV00024B/65/P

9 780578 407326